THE
FLAMING
CORSAGE

ALSO BY WILLIAM KENNEDY

The Ink Truck
Legs
Billy Phelan's Greatest Game
Ironweed
Quinn's Book
Very Old Bones

NONFICTION
O Albany!
Improbable City of Political Wizards, Fearless Ethnics,
Spectacular Aristocrats, Splendid Nobodies,
and Underrated Scoundrels
Riding the Yellow Trolley Car

WITH BRENDAN KENNEDY
Charlie Malarkey and the Belly Button Machine
Charlie Malarkey and the Singing Moose

THE
FLAMING
CORSAGE

William Kennedy

Viking

VIKING
Published by the Penguin Group
Penguin Books USA Inc., 375 Hudson Street,
New York, New York 10014, U.S.A.
Penguin Books Ltd, 27 Wrights Lane,
London W8 5TZ, England
Penguin Books Australia Ltd, Ringwood,
Victoria, Australia
Penguin Books Canada Ltd, 10 Alcorn Avenue,
Toronto, Ontario, Canada M4V 3B2
Penguin Books (N.Z.) Ltd, 182–190 Wairau Road,
Auckland 10, New Zealand

Penguin Books Ltd, Registered Offices:
Harmondsworth, Middlesex, England

First published in 1996 by Viking Penguin,
a division of Penguin Books USA Inc.

10   9   8   7   6   5   4   3   2   1

Copyright © WJK Inc., 1996
All rights reserved

LIBRARY OF CONGRESS CATALOGING-IN-PUBLICATION DATA
Kennedy, William.
    The flaming corsage : a novel / William Kennedy.
       p.   cm.
    ISBN 0-670-85872-2
    I. Title
PS3561.E428F53 1996
813'.54—dc20   95-49081

This book is printed on acid-free paper.
∞

Printed in the United States of America
Set in Cochin
Designed by Junie Lee

Here's a how-de-do!
If I marry you,
When your time has come to perish,
Then the maiden whom you cherish
Must be slaughtered, too!
Here's a how-de-do!
. . . . . .

With a passion that's intense
I worship and adore,
But the laws of common sense
We oughtn't to ignore.
If what he says is true,
'Tis death to marry you!
Here's a pretty state of things!
Here's a pretty how-de-do!

—Gilbert and Sullivan, The Mikado

THE
FLAMING
CORSAGE

THE LOVE NEST

October 17, 1908

WHEN THE HUSBAND made his surprise entrance into the
Manhattan hotel suite, his wife was leaning against a table, clad in a floor-length, forest-green velvet cloak, and
wearing a small eye mask of the same color, her black
hair loose to below her shoulders.

The second woman, her light-brown hair upswept
into a fuss of soft curls that bespoke an energetic nature,
and wearing a floor-length, peach-colored evening gown
embroidered with glass pearls, was in conversation with
the man who had rented this suite months earlier, and
who at this moment was wearing a frock coat, evening
trousers, wing collar, gray ascot and pearl stickpin, the
two dressed as if for a social evening. They were standing near the window that gave a view at dusk of the falling leaves and barren branches of the elms and maples of
lower Fifth Avenue.

The husband's entrance to the suite was made with a
key. How he came into possession of the key has not been
discovered. The husband spoke first to his wife, saying,
according to one witness, "You Babylonian whore, ev-

erything is undone"; or, according to the other witness, "Babylon, *regina peccatorum,* you are gone." Turning then to both the man in the wing collar and the second woman, the husband spoke of "traitors" and "vixen," his exact phrase unclear to both witnesses. The husband then opened his coat, drew a .45-caliber Colt revolver from his waistband, parted his wife's cloak with its barrel, placed the barrel against her left breast, and shot her precisely through the heart. The position in which she fell onto the carpet revealed that she wore nothing beneath the cloak.

The husband turned to the man by the window and fired two shots at him, hitting him with one, the force of which propelled him backward into the windowpane, which shattered. The second woman screamed, ran into the bedroom, and locked its door. The wounded man watched the husband staring at his pistol and heard him mumble, "Confido et conquiesco," which translates from the Latin as: I trust and am at peace. After saying this, the husband put the revolver barrel under his chin, pulled the trigger, and fell dead beside his exposed wife.

EDWARD IN THE CITY
OF TENTS

September 1885

IT WAS THE year the State Fair came to Albany, and as Edward
Daugherty walked through the vast city of tents and impromptu
structures that had sprung up in a matter of weeks at the Fairgrounds on the Troy Road, he felt a surge of strength, a certainty
that he was changing substantially, at the breaking dawn of a creative future.

He could see the tents on the midway where seven newspapers
had their offices and seven sets of reporters wrote yards of daily
copy about Shorthorns and Clydesdales, Cotswold sheep, and Po-
land China swine. In the *Albany Evening Journal*'s tent he found
Maginn writing at a table.

"What news do you have of the swine?" Edward asked.

"What a coincidence that you ask," Maginn said, and he thrust
what he was writing at Edward, who read:

> *Country maidens in their best bib and tucker shot coy glances at*
> *robust lads of brawny arm and sun-browned face as a brilliantly*
> *sunny day brought thousands to the midway of the Fair yester-*
> *day. Flirtations were numerous and many lords of creation suc-*
> *cumbed before batteries of sparkling eyes.*

"Splendid," said Edward, "but what about the swine?"

"They are the swine," said Maginn.

Edward was twenty-six, dark-haired and tall, considered by women young and old to be the handsomest of men. Thomas Maginn, lanky and lean at twenty-eight, was considered a ragtail beanpole with an acid tongue. The two worked for rival Albany newspapers, Maginn on *The Journal,* Edward on *The Argus,* had known each other a year, but now, as working rivals on the Fair's midway—better than a circus, as all knew—they had tested each other's attitudes toward this instant city and were impressed with its two miles of stables, its racetrack, its complete farm, its vast Hall of Machinery with the latest thermostatic chicken incubators, potato diggers, sulky plows, and type-writers, the oyster pavilion, the temporary lockup/courtroom where troublemakers won swift justice, and the curiosities—the solid-silver razor, the huge pyramid of sacked salt, the embalmed dog in a casket.

"A confected metropolis," Maginn had called the Fair, and Edward agreed that its rapid construction, and its appeal to both the elite and the crowd, reflected a creativity that could harmonize the wonders of existence with a flick of the mind. To such creation both young men aspired, seeing themselves as citizens of a world beyond newspapers. Edward had graduated with honors from Albany Academy and Columbia College. Maginn had been expelled from Columbia for drunkenness in his sophomore year, an autodidact ever since.

"Luckiest day of my life when they kicked me out," he said. "Unburdened forever of pedants and pederasts."

One night after the Fair closed, Maginn cajoled Edward into joining him at the Freethinkers convention at the Leland Opera House in Albany for a lecture on "The Aristocracy of Free Thought," and they heard a man named Palmer aver that "a true gentleman would always embrace the highest forms of culture and contribute most to the good of his fellowmen. And the true gentleman will maintain that woman's consent is as requisite as man's."

"I don't know as that's necessary," Maginn whispered.

"The best must rule," Palmer declaimed. "No man can prevail among the true elect if he remains imprisoned in the bastille of a dwarfing environment."

Just such an environment, Maginn said, he and Edward inhabited as Albany newsmen, but only temporarily. Edward was about to publish a novel, *The Mosquito Lovers* (about Irish convict laborers as expendable martyrs in the building of the Erie Canal, men who elected to risk a dig through malarial swampland rather than rot their souls in jail). Maginn regularly published reviews of fiction and belles lettres in the *Atlantic Monthly,* had just finished revaluing Melville's *The Confidence-Man* as an underrated work on human treachery, and was writing a novel.

This imminence of large-minded success convinced the young men they were vastly smarter than the run of Fairgoers, including their fellow reporters, and would soon inhabit a lofty perch in America's high culture. Maginn had shown Edward his Melville essay. Edward's response was "Well written but perfunctory. It would improve if you didn't view your own opinions as unmatched in human thought." Edward let Maginn read his novel in manuscript. Maginn found it "seriously wanting as fiction, but you write such effective dialogue you should be a playwright."

This critical honesty formed a bond of truth-telling between them, and their friendship deepened when they found they could talk to each other about anything at all.

As they strolled the trim rolling field that came down from the western rise of the valley, they eyed passing females and tried to recall all women they had ever desired. Maginn observed that a voluptuous woman was the greatest gift the universe offered to an imaginative man, a statement that seemed true to Edward; but the word "voluptuous," "How do you define it, Maginn?"

"A woman who delights in her body and what a man does to it," said Maginn. "A woman who loves the encounter."

"You mean a *loose* woman, then?"

"Not quite, but all women are loose at some time or other," Maginn said.

"I disagree," Edward said. "The most voluptuous woman I've ever met I know in my soul isn't promiscuous, and is undoubtedly a virgin."

"They become loose after they cease to be virgins."

"You are very down on women."

"Every chance I get," said Maginn.

"I may marry a woman who doesn't conform to your view of promiscuous females." Then, without wishing to, but in defense of his putative bride-to-be, he blurted out her name: "Katrina Taylor."

"Katrina Taylor! She said yes to you?"

"Not yet. I'm waiting for her answer."

"You are one extraordinarily lucky son of a bitch if you snare her, my friend. She's a woman in a million. I met her last February skating on the canal, but I doubt she knows my name."

"She may not have me," Edward said.

"Ye gods! Katrina Taylor! Thinking about a woman like that must drive you mad. What do you do when the urge comes on you?"

"Which urge? I have many."

"The only urge worth yielding to. It's on me now just talking about women, and I thought I'd yield over at the Pasture."

"The Pasture?"

"You are benighted, Daugherty. You've been here a week and haven't heard of the *other* tent city? We must complete your education."

As dusk enveloped the Fairgrounds and the Fair's seven gates closed for the night, the young men walked to the Bull's Head tavern, beyond the fenced pasture where six bulls rested beside a barn. They walked across the tavern's open meadow, where prizefights were staged, to four small tents standing in a clearing of the bordering woods. This was the Fair-spawned Night Village, where the Ladies of the Pasture sold bucolic love. The brothels downtown in Albany and across the river in Troy were servicing multitudes of visiting Fairgoers in quest of passion's two-bit nocturne; but the higher-paid Ladies of the Pasture opened for business at high noon and worked well past moonrise, catering to postmeridian libido, and to lust which lacked the time or inclination to quit the Fair's environs.

The night was brisk and Edward and Maginn both wore fedoras and three-button suits. A man sitting in front of one open tent lit by a kerosene lamp was accepting money from a tall, brawny farm boy. The boy paid, then bent himself into the tent and closed the flap behind him.

"You boys in the market?"

"We're shopping," said Maginn.

"Anything in particular?"

"They should be pretty."

"Hell, they're all pretty once you're in that tent. Just go say hello and see what you like. Last three tents. The first one's busy."

"We'll take a look," Maginn said.

As he and Edward walked to the farthest tent, Edward stopped and asked aloud, "Why am I doing this?"

"What is it you're doing?"

"I don't know."

"Then you're making a discovery," Maginn said. "Like Lewis and Clark charting the Northwest Territory, we're about to enter the heady hemisphere of love."

"I'm already in love."

"Love may look virginal, but also whorish. You have to differentiate the forms."

"This will serve me well?"

"You will earn medals for your service."

"Who awards the medals?"

"The whores of the world, by which I mean most of the human race."

"You have a dark view of life, Maginn."

"Dark, like French pussy," Maginn said.

At the last tent Maginn raised the flap and they walked in on two young whores who looked about twenty, bundled in coats, sitting on chairs.

"Good evening, ladies, we came to say hello."

"Is that all you came for?" asked the one with blond bangs and a crossed eye.

"We'd like to see what you're offering."

The girls stood and took off their coats, showing matching bodies clad in chemisettes and black stockings.

"My name is Nellie," said the girl with normal eyes, lowering her shoulder strap. She was dark-haired and chesty. "We came to see the Fair," she said.

"And have you seen it?"

"Not yet. We found this job, and when we get through at night the Fair is closed."

"Well, we're glad *you're* not closed," Maginn said. "You look lovely from the anterior perspective, but may we now have your posterior revelation?"

"What's that?" the cross-eyed girl asked.

"He means our fannies," Nellie said. The two turned their backs and bent from the waist.

"Very intriguing," Maginn said. "We'll be back."

"Thank you kindly, girls," Edward said.

"Don't mention it," Nellie said, and she raised the front of her chemisette for Edward. Maginn pulled Edward by the arm outside and toward the next tent.

"She was nice," Edward said.

"Not bad for starters," Maginn said, "but we shouldn't accept the first offer."

"What if you like the offer?"

"You're fond of busty women."

"I liked her style."

"She lacks all style. What you like is subliterate quim."

"Whatever you call it, it's worth some attention."

"Take a squint here first," Maginn said, and he opened the tent flap. A woman in her thirties, her long brown hair streaked with gray, smiled at her visitors. She was sitting on her cot, wrapped in a blanket, only her black stockings visible.

"You boys looking to get warm?"

"Maybe even hot," Maginn said.

"That can happen," the whore said, and she stood and spread her arms to open the blanket. "Here's the stove."

She had penetrating eyes that gave her face a smartness Edward liked. She wasn't as chesty as Nellie, but ample, and her symmetry raised the issue of sexual aesthetics in Edward's brain.

"I wish we had a camera," he said.

"Camera ain't what you point at this," the whore said.

"What should we point at it?" Maginn asked.

"You really asking me that question?"

"He's making a joke," Edward said.

"I ain't here for jokes."

"I apologize for him. How much do you charge?"

"Six bits, same as the others, unless I do more. You know what I mean?"

"I guess I do," Edward said.

"I guess you don't, if you gotta guess about it."

"What's your name?" Edward asked.

"Rose," the whore said. "And I got the pink petals to prove it."

"I think I'll stay," Edward said.

"There's another tent to check out," Maginn said.

"You check it and give me a report. I'm with Rose."

"That's my cute boy," Rose said.

"All right, since you insist," Maginn said. "I'll meet you in the tavern in fifteen minutes."

"Fifteen minutes?" said Edward. "What if it's two hours?"

"You take two hours," Rose said, "you get your money back." She unbuttoned Edward's suit coat.

"Don't wait for me past Tuesday," Edward told Maginn.

Edward wondered at his own choice, decided he was behaving instinctually, without accessible logic, but knew his behavior was full of awe and pity and reverence and some bizarre desire yet to be understood. As Rose moved through her early performance Edward adjudged her a woman of imaginative display: skilled in revelation, exalted by self-communion, who yielded herself without haste. "A gift of flint, nest of tinder" is how he would describe such a woman in one of his short stories. She moved Edward slowly into fervency.

"Tell Rose you like her and you're gonna take her."

"I like Rose so much I'm taking her for a ride."

"That's my cute boy."

"This train is moving."

"All aboard. Going home to your best girl."

"Rose is my best girl."

"Rose is the only girl you ever wanted."

"Rose is there from the first day."

"You couldn't go no place without Rose."

"We're going to heaven, me and Rose."

"This boy is so nice that Rose is in love."

"I'm in love with Rose."

"The cute boy's in love with an old whore."

"Rose isn't old."

"The cute boy's in love with an ugly old whore."

"I'm in love with a beautiful whore named Rose."

"The cute boy makes Rose happy."

"Is Rose happy making love?"

"Rose is happy making money."

"Which comes first, the money or the love?"

"They all come before Rose."

"Gotta go, Rose."

"Not yet, cute boy."

"Rose is so nice it's nice, but I'm going away."

"It's not two hours."

"Two hours couldn't be better than now."

"My cute boy."

"Goodbye, Rose."

"There goes the cute boy."

"There goes Rose."

"Cute boy is gone."

"And Rose?"

"Rose is where she is."

At the crowded bar in the Bull's Head tavern, Maginn greeted Edward with a triumphant smile.

"Two for the price of one," he said. "I went back to the first tent and opted for the bung-eyed bitch, but she was so lackadaisical I departed her corpus and threatened not to pay for such inertia. Her tenting twin—Nellie, wasn't it?—came to the rescue. Very vigorous, Nellie. Bicameral bawds. Unexpected dividend. How was Rose?"

"Splendid."

"In what way?"

"In all ways."

"You went all ways?"

"She was splendid. Let it go at that."

"The details are important, Daugherty. As a reporter you should know that."

"This place is too noisy," Edward said. The bar was two deep with drinkers, fogged with cigar and pipe smoke, and in a corner a fight seemed about to happen. "Let's go someplace quiet. I'm hungry."

"Venereal delight stokes the appetite."

They took the West Shore train from the Fairgrounds to downtown Albany, and at Edward's insistence walked up from the station to the Kenmore for dinner.

"I can't afford their prices," Maginn said. "I'm not yet part of the plutocracy, like some of my friends."

"It's good that I am," Edward said. "I'll buy dinner."

"Done," said Maginn. "A plutocratic gesture if there ever was one."

In addition to wages from *The Argus*, Edward had an annuity from birth given to him by Lyman Fitzgibbon that would keep him from starving until he reached age thirty, four years hence, and this allowed him to keep rooms on Columbia Street, close to the newspaper and just up from the Kenmore, where, unlike Maginn, he dined often.

He went to the men's washroom and soaped off the residue of Rose's body from his hands and his privates. Then he went back upstairs and with Maginn sat in the tan leather chairs of the hotel's lobby lounge while they waited for a table. Maginn bought a cigar at the newsstand, bit off the end and spat it into the brass cuspidor, then lit the cigar with a match he struck on the sole of Edward's shoe.

Edward saw Katrina entering with her parents through the hotel's side door on Columbia Street, avoiding the lobby and the vulgar stares of the loungers. The three went directly to the dining room—reserved table, of course.

"Isn't that the magnificent woman you proposed to?" Maginn asked.

"That is she. With Mama and Papa."

"Her beauty is exhilarating."

"I agree."

"I wonder how she compares with Rose."

"Wonder to yourself," Edward said.

"Protective already," said Maginn. "I can see the transformation. 'Once the favorite of whores of all ages, Edward Daugherty has evolved into the perfect husband.' "

Edward perceived that Maginn, the gangling whoremonger, was miffed that women in both tents had given their preferred eye to

Edward; and he would, in a later year, remember this day as the beginning of his relationship to Maginn's envy and self-esteem, the beginning of competitive lives, even to evaluating the predilections of whores ("They picked you because you picked them, no trick to that"). It would be Maginn's oft-repeated credo that "the only thing that can improve on a lovely whore is another lovely whore." Edward's unspoken credo toward Katrina-as-bride-to-be was: "If she becomes my wife, then my wife is my life."

The Kenmore's maître d', a light-skinned Negro, came toward them. "Your table is ready, Mr. Daugherty," he said.

"Very good, Walter."

He led them to a table next to Katrina and her parents. But Edward asked for one at the far end of the crowded dining room, Albany's largest, where Parlatti's orchestra was playing a medley from Gilbert and Sullivan's *The Mikado,* all the rage.

"I'd like to meet your bride formally," Maginn said. "Will you introduce me?"

"Another time. And she's not yet my bride."

They walked past the Taylors without a glance. After they'd been seated beside a thicket of potted palms, Edward walked back and greeted Katrina, Geraldine, and Jacob Taylor. He stared at Katrina, her golden hair swept into an almost luminous soft corona, and was about to bend and kiss her hand; but then he thought of his mouth on Rose's body, and only bent and nodded and smiled his love toward her.

"Your friend Giles Fitzroy won two gold medals today at the Fair, for his saddle horses," Edward said to her.

"The Fitzroys do breed champions," Jacob Taylor said.

"I've been reading what you write about the Fair," Katrina said. "You make it so exciting. I want to see it."

The sound of her voice, the cadence of her speech, seemed musical to Edward, a fragment of a Mozart aria. Everything about her had the aura of perfection. He knew his perception must be awry, and he thought he should try to find flaws in the woman. But to what end? Is it so wrong to embrace perfection? Am I a dunce to believe in it?

"Come tomorrow," he said. "I'll give you an insider's tour. You come with her, Geraldine; you, too, Jake."

"I think not," Geraldine Taylor said. "I'm told it's overrun with a vulgar crowd."

"There are some of those," Edward said, and he understood that Geraldine could accept no generosity, not even a meaningless invitation, if it came from beneath her station.

"People like the Fitzroys and the Parkers and the Cornings are exhibitors," Edward said, "and they're frequently around. I'll stop by in the morning, Katrina, and see what you decide." He nodded farewell and went back to Maginn, who was buttering a biscuit as a waiter poured his wine.

"I sit here and look at these good burghers with their gold watch chains dangling over their pus bellies," Maginn said, "and I all but drown in my loathing."

"That's juvenile," said Edward. "They're only people who've found a way to make some money."

"Come on now, Edward. They're another breed. With them and us it's like thoroughbreds and swine. Those mosquito-loving Irish canal diggers in your novel are sewer rats to them. But I loathe them just as much as they loathe me. Is there *one of them* in this dining room who'd invite you home if they knew you drink in a saloon that has an encampment of whores in the backyard? Or me—if they found out my old man salvages hides and bones of dead horses and sells their flesh to pig farmers?"

"I would," said Edward.

"You're a rare specimen," said Maginn, "and I drink to whatever makes you say that." He sipped his wine, put down the glass. "But then you still tote the baggage of the sentimental mick, offering alms to forlorn souls. You're really not that long out of the bog yourself, are you?"

"Long enough that I'm at home in this room, no matter what company I keep."

"Touché. Yet you wouldn't introduce me to Katrina. Too obvious a bogtrotter, is that my problem?"

"It's a family situation. Let's move on to something else, shall we?"

Edward imagined Maginn unloosing his gutter candor in the presence of Katrina and her parents, and he winced. Just what Geraldine expects from the Irish. Maginn, you're great company, and you own a fine mind, but you are a problem.

"You keep complaining about your editor at *The Journal,*" Edward said. "How do you get along with him?"

"Like a tree gets along with a dog."

"If you're interested, I'll put in a word at *The Argus.* I know my editor would like to have your lively style in our pages. He's said as much."

"My present editor loathes my lively style."

"There's a lot of loathing in your life, Maginn."

"You connect me at *The Argus,* my loathing will dissipate like warm sunshine lifting fog off a bog."

"I'll do what I can."

"You're a princely fellow, Daugherty, a princely fellow, for a mick. I'll buy the wine."

EDWARD REDISCOVERS
KATRINA

November 1884

EDWARD HAD ENTERED Katrina's world at the adolescent moment
when he registered at Albany Academy to begin the education
Lyman Fitzgibbon, Geraldine Taylor's father, had ordained for
him. Edward's father, Emmett Daugherty, came to this country
from County Galway in 1836 at age fourteen, and at eighteen
hired on as coachman for Lyman's Adirondack expedition, an extended trip to acquire land for the railroad, lumbering, and mining
interests that were central to Lyman's bountiful life. The expedition encountered hostility in a remote Warren County hamlet that
was so new it lacked a name. Lyman and his lawyer were taken
captive by townsmen, who foresaw accurately that these interlop-
ers were about to change life as they knew it; and they prepared
tar and feathers for them. Young Emmett Daugherty, as truculent
as the next man when called upon, picked up a fallen tree branch
and felled the townsmen's ringleader, then garroted him with a
horsewhip and, by legend, told the man's cronies, "Turn those men
loose or I twist the tongue out of his head," the tongue already
halfway out.

That was July 1840, and Lyman vowed Emmett would never

want for anything again, and that his children would have the best education available.

Edward was born to Emmett and Hanorah Sweeney on Main Street in the North End in 1859, went to the North End public school for five years, then three years to the Christian Brothers boys' school on Colonie Street in Arbor Hill, Emmett insisting that Edward first discover the workingman's God before going off to study among pagans and Protestants.

Lyman Fitzgibbon was London-born (1805), Oxford-educated, a translator of Tacitus' *Germania*, wealthy early in life, a British diplomat at midlife, and, as British consul in France, rescuer of Louis-Philippe in the revolution of 1848. For his inventions relating to metalworking machinery he was called "the merchant-scientist" and, along with his stove-making foundry and investments, he became not only Albany's richest man, but its most variously eminent. He was also Edward's godfather.

Through the benediction of this eminence, Edward, when he enrolled in the Academy, entered the elite circle of Albany's social life, became close friends with boys whose fathers ran the city, was invited to dances with debutantes, sleigh rides and tobogganing expeditions out to the Albany County Club, and dinners at the Fort Orange Club as Lyman's guest. On such occasions he came to know the young Katrina Taylor, Lyman's granddaughter, but she was six years his junior, a child. They grew up as friendly "common-law cousins," as he called their relationship. They were separated by Edward's years at Columbia College, when he lived in New York City, and later by his western trip to research the lives of the Irish workers who had built the Erie, men whose achievement his father had invoked often, and about whom Edward was writing his first novel. And so it was not until the night the Democrats marched in the vast torchlight parade celebrating Cleveland's defeat of Blaine in the presidential election that Edward encountered the maturing Katrina.

The city was explosive with lights, bonfires, fireworks, and parties to hail the new chief of state from Albany, and a line of thousands of marchers, their oil-lit torches creating a dancing serpent of lights, moved past more thousands of cheering spectators in a triumphal procession up State Street's steep incline. Edward watched from the stoop of Lyman's home, an august four-and-a-half-story brownstone facing on State Street and, like other homes on this night, festooned with Chinese lanterns. More lanterns bloomed like bizarre forms of fruit on Lyman's trees, and buildings across the street displayed the American and Irish flags, and huge images of Grover Cleveland.

In the crowd on the sidewalk a woman caught Edward's eye when she opened a yellow parasol and held it aloft over her yellow bonnet as the parade approached. The band played and the marchers yelled in left-right cadence: "Blaine, Blaine, James G. Blaine, the continental liar from the state of Maine," and Edward recognized the woman with the yellow bonnet as Katrina. He went down the stoop and stood behind her and patted her shoulder. When she turned to him he saw a Katrina (she was "Katch" to him as a child) he'd never known.

"My God, how lovely you look, Katch," he said. "What have you done to yourself? You're positively beautiful."

"I suppose I've grown up. But so have you. You look very much a man of the world, Edward."

"And so I like to think that I am. But even as a man of the world I don't understand why you open your parasol when it is neither sunny nor raining."

"It well might rain oil on my new bonnet from those dreadful torches. And I would not like that at all."

The marchers broke into a new chant: "Ma, Ma, where's my Pa?" a Blaine campaign slogan about Cleveland's bastard son. But the electorate shrugged off this scandal, and the marchers now voiced the new, answering gibe: "Gone to the White House, ha, ha, ha!"

"That is so funny, and so just," Katrina said.

"Didn't his fathering a child out of wedlock scandalize you?"

"He never denied the boy, and he took care of him. He's a courageous man, Mr. Cleveland."

"You have a modern outlook on the matter, for a woman."

"I am a modern woman."

"So you say. And so you may be."

Katrina spotted Giles Fitzroy riding with a dozen men from the Jacksonians. She called his name and waved to him.

"It's Giles," she said. "He's riding Phantom Guest. What a beautiful horse. This is all so wonderful. We really, really won. It's staggering, isn't it?"

"Cleveland owes his election to me, did you know that?"

"No, you must tell me. Did you vote a thousand times?"

"Not quite. Are you going to Lyman's party?"

"Of course."

"Then I'll tell you there."

They watched the paraders: all the Democratic clubs, many carrying brooms for a clean sweep, and the Irish-American Association (with which Emmett Daugherty marched), and the German Democratic Business Men, the Dry Goods Cleveland Club stepping to the rhythms of the Tenth Infantry Band, and the Flynn Fife and Drum Corps, and so many more, moving up to Capitol Park, where the President-elect waved down from his executive chamber.

When all paraders had passed, Edward and Katrina went into Lyman's house, where bustling servants were setting out punch bowls and placing vases of flowers on tables and mantels.

"We're early," Edward said, and he greeted the servants and steered Katrina by the arm into the conservatory. She sat on a bench with her parasol in her lap, and Edward looked long at her and studied the phenomenal change in her face, the way she combed her hair, the way she held herself with such poise, such an air of certainty about who and what she was.

"You are dazzling tonight, Katch," he said. "How old are you now?"

"I'm about to be nineteen, thank you."

"Is anybody paying court to your radiant self?"

"I have my admirers."

"Permit me to join their number. Where have I been?"

"You should control yourself and tell me how you elected the President."

He leaned on the back of her bench and put his eyes in line with hers. Looking at her face silenced him.

"Well?" she said.

"Yes, the election. I'd much rather look at you. I went to a dinner party at the Fort Orange Club to meet the Governor, and Lyman introduced me as 'the talented son of a fine Irishman whose vote you need.' Mr. Cleveland agreed the Irish vote was important and asked who my father might be.

" 'Emmett Daugherty, foreman at Lyman's foundry,' I told him, 'but I doubt he'll vote for you, Governor. He's very angry with all politicians, and so is the whole North End. Father Loonan, the pastor of Sacred Heart church, talks of it every Sunday from the pulpit, and a North End saloonkeeper with a keen political eye says his customers are talking Blaine. North Enders are Democrats, but this year it's up for grabs.'

" 'Why are they so angry with me?' the Governor asked me.

" 'You, the Mayor, the aldermen, everybody who forces them to live in mud,' I said. 'Anybody who hasn't delivered any pavement to North Albany's streets or sidewalks. It's an old, old promise nobody's ever kept. They see Elk Street, where your wealthy friends live, being paved with granite blocks, while they're still riding on rotting planks in a sea of mud. After a rain they have to put bog shoes on their horses to get home. And they blame you.'

" 'Do you know Father Loonan?' says the Governor.

" 'I do,' says I.

" 'Bring him and this saloonkeeper—what's his name?'

" 'Jack McCall. Black Jack, they call him.'

" 'Bring Black Jack and the good father up to see me. We'll have a chat.'

" 'I'll do that tomorrow,' says I.

" 'Do you know anybody else who doesn't like me?' the Governor says.

" 'Aren't the North End Irish enough?' says I.

"I had no trouble convincing Jack and Father Loonan to visit the Governor. He saw us straightaway and had Mayor Banks in the office with him. They listened to the complaints about mud and the Governor asked the Mayor could he get the contractor paving Elk Street to start on Broadway in North Albany? The Mayor said the city had let no contract to pave Broadway.

" 'Well, *let* one,' said the Governor. 'We'll get you reimbursed. But get the crews out there tomorrow.' And the Mayor said he'd get on it.

"The Governor thanked me for my enterprise; then he and Black Jack got off on fishing and it was as if they'd known each other forever. 'We'll have to go to the mountains one day and get some trout,' the Governor said, and on the way out Father Loonan told me I ought to run for governor when Cleveland leaves. I said I couldn't, that I was a writer.

"The next day, workers put granite blocks on Broadway, starting in front of Sacred Heart church. We had a rally five nights later and five hundred heard Jack's speech. They marched and chanted against Blaine, the highway robber from the state of Maine. It was the biggest political turnout in neighborhood history. And Blaine's support went the way of North Albany mud.

"Cleveland carried the state by one thousand one hundred and forty-nine votes," Edward said. "Only five hundred and seventy-five votes would have reversed those results, and the Democratic plurality in North Albany was six hundred and seventy-seven."

"Why, you're a miracle worker," Katrina said.

"I'm glad you understand that about me," Edward said.

People were arriving from the parade, and Lyman's valet was helping him down the stairs to the parlor to greet them.

"He looks so frail lately," Katrina said.

"Only his body. His mind is very astute."

"He's terribly fond of you," Katrina said.

"He's like a second father," Edward said. "And he's crazy about you. But right this minute I'm crazier about you than he is."

"You are turning this girl's head, sir."

"I mean to do nothing else, as soon as I'm able. I have obligations for a month or two."

"I'm abandoned before I'm courted."

"You will not be abandoned. I intend to pursue you with a fervid Irish passion, unlike anything you've ever imagined. But I must finish what I've begun."

"And what is it you've begun?"

"A novel I've been writing for more than a year, the key to my new life. One key. You are the other."

"You've become an impetuous man, Edward."

"I am a man instantly in love. Do you mind if I love you?"

"I have never been so flattered, or so quickly."

"I have just begun to flatter you. I have just begun to worship you."

EDWARD BEGINS A SERIOUS DIALOGUE WITH KATRINA, WHILE DANCING

September 1885

IN THE MONTHS that followed his rediscovery of Katrina, Edward took a leave from *The Argus* and devoted his days to the final research and writing of his Erie Canal novel. He finished by late summer 1885, and began, with great earnestness, a campaign to have himself invited to all social events he knew Katrina would attend. Katrina's mother noted this.

"That man is a pest," Geraldine said.

"He's a perfect gentleman, and very intelligent," Katrina said. "I'm always happy to see him."

"I don't care how intelligent he is, he's not the right sort for you," her mother said.

September's major social event was the ball for the coming-out of Felicity Grenville, held in Bleecker Hall on Maiden Lane. Edward found Katrina besieged by suitors and only at the cotillion did he discover she had saved a place for him on her dance card. As soon as they were arm in arm in the dance he said to her, "I've decided. Yes, I've made the decision."

"Oh? And what did you decide?"

"To ask you to marry me."

"I believe I knew that."

"Wasn't that presumptuous of you?"

"I'm a student of love, Edward, and you seem to be a proper subject for my scrutiny."

"You considered my proposal even before you heard it."

"I wouldn't have dared."

"But in your scrutiny you had passing thoughts. Is your answer yes?"

"No."

"Is it no?"

"I don't think so."

"Not a very satisfactory response."

"You have no right to an instant answer to that question."

"But you expected the question."

"Yes, but I must confirm the reality."

"How do you do that?"

"By testing myself. For instance, how do I know if I should marry you when I haven't even kissed you?"

"I could rectify that immediately. Here and now."

"It would cause a scandal. 'Woe be to him who gives scandal to my brethren.' "

"Upstairs, then? Downstairs? Outside?"

"If it happens, I don't want even the birds to see."

"I'll find a secret place where we can be alone."

"I'll find it when the time is right," Katrina said.

EDWARD AND THE BEAN SOUP

September 25, 1885

EDWARD WALKED THE three miles up Broadway from *The Argus* to Black Jack's saloon, marking the trail through the North End with whatever psychic spoor it is that would-be bridegrooms create when they make plans to abandon home territory. He came to where the pavement used to abruptly end: at the carriageway into the pasture of the Patroon's Manor House (where his mother had worked as a cook for the last Patroon's widow). The Manor House was the northern boundary of civilization as Albany's roadbuilders judged it, and after it you entered the wild Irish neighborhood where Edward was raised, and for which plank roads and mud had sufficed.

Now new granite pavement continued past the Manor entrance, past the gasworks. And where the molders and lumber handlers of the North End had built their houses, slate sidewalks covered the old dirt paths. It pleased Edward to have been partially responsible for this, though the public heroes of upgraded life were Father Loonan and especially Jack McCall, who, in return for staging the rally that reversed the voting slide toward Blaine, had been named Democratic Leader of the Ninth Ward.

Jack had been born into saloon life. His father, Butter McCall, ran the Bull's Head tavern on the Troy Road until his liver stiffened, whereupon he sold the place, outraging Jack, who considered the Bull's Head his future; so Jack then opened his own saloon on Broadway, now headquarters for anyone seeking favor with the Democratic party.

"Short one," Edward said to Jack, who was talking to Maginn. Jack, behind the bar in white apron and collarless white shirt, was a formidable presence, thick head of hair, Roman nose, clean-shaven, and muscular from hefting beer barrels, first at the Bull's Head, then for the Quinn and Nolan brewery. The time now in Black Jack's saloon was the lull before the invasion at six when the lumber mills' whistles would blow the twelve-hour workday into oblivion, and those handlers with money to quaff would move single-mindedly into liquid pleasure. The remains of the bean soup simmered in the pot on the woodstove behind the bar, half emptied by the lunch crowd; the ham was getting down to the bone; the bread growing stale; but soup, ham, and bread would all be eaten by six-thirty, and the hell with food after that hour, was Jack's dictum.

Edward, when marriage became a possibility, had thought of Jack for his best man, and his visit here today was to tell Jack of his proposal to Katrina, and the resistance he was meeting from her parents. Finding Maginn here was a surprise. Maginn, now reporting for *The Argus*, was at the end of the bar behind his new mustache, his suit hanging loosely on his lanky frame. He was talking to Jack, pumping him about the invitation he'd received from his newfound friend, the President of the United States, to go fishing. The election poster for Cleveland and Hendricks dominated the wall of the back bar.

"He telling his White House fish story?" Edward asked.

"He's telling about the letter," Maginn said.

"He wants the mountains," Jack said. "Trout he wants. 'Pick any place in the Adirondacks,' he tells me."

"And what did you pick?"

"North Creek. They got trout up there big as dogs. They jump out of the water to shake hands."

"That'll be some circus, fishing with the President," Edward said.

"No it won't," said Jack. "We won't tell anybody where we're gonna light. He don't want a circus, he wants to fish."

"I know how important the President is," Maginn said, "but did you hear this young lad here may soon be stretched on the holy rack of matrimony."

"No," said Jack. "Is that true?"

"It could be true," Edward said. "But there are things to be done."

"Buy the bed and spread the sheets, he means," said Maginn. "He's marrying up. Beautiful, smart, and rich. Altogether too much for him."

"Too much for me, but just enough for Maginn, if he could only get his hands on her."

"Who is she? Not Ruthie."

"No, not Ruthie," Edward said.

"Does Ruthie know?"

"No. It's Jake Taylor's daughter Katrina. I proposed. She hasn't said yes yet."

"Jake Taylor? That royal son of a bitch. What's Emmett say to that?"

"He doesn't know about it either, but he won't relish it."

"He wouldn't, after Davy."

"Davy?" said Maginn.

"My father's brother," Edward said. "Jake's goons beat him so bad when he tried to organize the lumber handlers, all he can do now is shovel sawdust."

Edward and Jack had courted the same girls (Ruthie was the last), fished, hunted birds, and played baseball together, lived in houses back-to-back, went to school together, and grew apart only when Edward left the Christian Brothers school and moved into Lyman's home downtown to be closer to Albany Academy.

"Jake's family's Protestant," Jack said.

"Very true," said Edward. Jack's look judged him a traitor.

"Where's the wedding gonna be at?"

"I haven't even talked to her parents yet."

"You worry about them?"

"She does."

"There's no problem," Maginn said. "Why should a mudhole

mick from the North End have any problem marrying into one of Albany's first families?"

"Who's a mudhole mick?"

The voice came from a table where two men had been eavesdropping on the presidential talk. The bigger of the two came over to Maginn. He wore a sweater and a cap, had the slouch of a man whose back had lifted too much weight, and his drooping right eye gave him a permanent squint. Edward knew him as Matty Lookup, a lumber handler and ice cutter on hard times, suspected of breaking into Benedict's lumber office in the District and stealing four rubber coats and pieces of harness; and so no one would hire him now. He had come by his name when he chased somebody into Tommy Mullon's icehouse on Erie Street and lost him, but three boys in the icehouse loft called out, "Look up, Matty, look up," and when he did they dumped a bag of horseshit on him.

"Who's a mudhole mick?" Matty Lookup said a second time.

"I don't remember," Maginn said.

"He's making a joke," Edward said. Always explaining Maginn's jokes.

"You calling me a mudhole mick?"

"I don't even know you," Maginn said. "Why would I call you anything?"

"You don't like the Irish?"

"I am Irish."

"You look like a goddamn Dutchman."

"I don't have enough money to be Dutch."

"You talk like you don't like the Irish."

"Why don't you go find a mudhole that'll accept you, and lay down and take a bath," Maginn said.

Matty Lookup grabbed Maginn's throat with both hands, lifted him off his stool, then off the floor, and swung him around like the ball of a hammer. While Maginn the splinter flailed helplessly with his fists (like pummeling a sack of grain), Jack came around the bar to pull the two apart but was staggered by Matty Lookup's backhanded wallop. Matty was pinning Maginn to a tabletop, positioning himself to bite off Maginn's right ear, when Edward vaulted the bar, lifted the cauldron of bean soup off Jack's stove with both hands, and moved with it toward the unequal struggle. He yelled in his most urgent vibrato, "Look up, Matty! Look up!" and, as Matty's teeth parted to release Maginn's ear and his glance turned predictably toward those mocking words, Edward hurled the boiling soup into his face; and Matty knew agony. He rolled off the table onto the sawdust of Black Jack's floor, screeching the song of the scalded beast. Edward stood over him, the pot raised above his head with both hands, ready to break the brute's skull if his belligerence revived. Matty wailed in pain and Edward lowered the pot. Jack, a short club in his right hand now, nudged Matty with his foot.

"Get out you crazy son of a bitch, get out," Jack told him. "Come in again, you'll get worse."

Matty Lookup, whimpering out of his ruined flesh, stood up and shuffled his crumpled form out the door.

"How's your ear?" Edward asked Maginn, who, with a handkerchief, was blotting the blood that oozed from his lightly chewed ear. "Did he eat much of it?"

"Don't worry about it," Maginn said. "I've got his nose in my pocket."

"You hurt any place?" Jack asked him. "I thought you were all done."

"I would've been, except for our nimble novelist here. Quick thinking, old man. I myself might've reached for a bottle to club him with, but I'd've never gone for the soup. A genteel weapon. Your prospective in-laws would doubtless approve the choice."

Don't say anything, Maginn.

Jack tapped Edward's arm with his club.

"Good, Eddie," he said. "You did good." Then he went behind the bar to get the mop.

The whistle blew in the Lumber District. Six o'clock. The men would be pouring in, any minute. Edward now hated this saloon, hated Matty Lookup, Matty Beansoup, Matty Noface, hated his own savage response to the oaf. What was served by your attack and your sacrifice, Matty? What rubric of resistance did I serve with the soup? He held the empty pot in his hand. He looked at it: foot and a half deep, blue enamel, chipped rim, charred bottom, implement of retribution. He looked up and saw Maginn staring at him and smiling, blotting soup from his coat. Jack came with the pail and mop and went to work on the beans.

Edward could not now ask Jack to be his best man. A great fellow, Jack. A generous man if ever there was one, and now he's got Ruthie all to himself. But he doesn't approve of Katrina. Everybody's generosity ends somewhere.

Maginn was still smiling.

"Shut up, Maginn," Edward said.

EDWARD DELIVERS A MANIFESTO

September 27, 1885

EDWARD MOUNTED THE stoop of Katrina's home on Elk Street, a quiet shaded thoroughfare on Capitol Hill that because of its monied residents was known as Quality Row. This was his first visit to this house since his proposal to Katrina. He'd seen her often, exchanged letters with her daily, but was *persona non grata* until her insistence wore down her parents. She had written Edward this morning that her determination had triumphed, that they would talk to him about the future; and so now, at afternoon, when he rang the pullbell of the Taylors' Gothic Revival town house, Fletcher, the family butler these ten years, opened the door to him. As Edward entered the foyer, Fletcher took his hat, put it on the hall hat rack.

"Miss Katrina will meet you in the library, Mr. Daugherty."

"Thank you, Fletcher. How goes the horseshoe season?"

Fletcher, a precise and florid man of some wit, and with a day laborer's constitution, was horseshoe champion of Elk Street servants. A summer-long competition ran in the court alongside the Taylor stables, and Edward, being of neither master nor servant class, occasionally joined the games.

"Somewhat predictably, sir," Fletcher said.

"You mean you're ahead."

"Yes, sir, I do mean that."

"I almost beat you last time," Edward said.

"You did, indeed. But, alas, you did not."

"My turn will come, Fletcher."

"It's always good to believe that, Mr. Daugherty."

Fletcher led him to the empty library and lighted the gas in the six globes of the chandelier. The library was part sitting room with tea table and cane-bottomed straight-backed chairs, walnut bookcases with glass doors and perhaps two hundred books, blue velvet drapes on the windows, and Jacob Taylor's orderly walnut desk, with two leather armchairs facing it. Edward sat in one of these chairs, staring at the books. He waited, listened to the silence of the vast house, stood and searched for two particular books he'd read when he came here with Lyman years ago. He scanned the English and Dutch history books, such a burden when he first opened them, and now they weighed on him again: all that confirmation of ancestry. But where are the books of *my* lineage, *my* ancient history? My history has not yet been written.

He found books on Albany's Dutch origins, volumes in the Dutch language, studies of the first Dutch and Episcopal churches of seventeenth-century Albany, lives of the Van Rensselaers, Albany's founding family and its dynasty of patroons, lives of the Staatses, Jacob's family, and shelves of Shakespeare, Dickens, Thackeray (which Katrina read avidly before she was allowed to have them), Washington's memoirs, *The Federalist Papers*, and books on the English in Ireland, yes: what Edward was seeking.

He took two volumes from the shelf and sat and skimmed them: "The Irish are abominable, false, cunning and perfidious people . . . The worst means of governing them is to give them their own way. In concession they see only fear, and those that fear them they hate and despise. Coercion succeeds better . . . they respect a master hand, though it be a hard and cruel one . . . Cromwell alone understood this . . ."

The same Cromwell, Lord Lieutenant of Ireland, writing of his 1649 attack on Drogheda: ". . . the enemy were about 3,000 strong in the town . . . I believe we put to the sword the whole number . . . I forbade them to spare any that were in arms in the Town . . .

about 200 of them possessed St. Peter's Church-steeple . . . I ordered the steeple . . . to be fired, when one of them was heard to say in the midst of the flames: 'God damn me, God confound me; I burn, I burn.' . . . I wish that all honest hearts may give the glory of this to God alone . . ."

And then to Wexford to slaughter 2,000 more: "I thought it not right or good to restrain off the soldiers from their right of pillage, or from doing execution on the enemy."

And Sir William Petty's estimates: that the war reduced Ireland's population from one million, four hundred and sixty-six thousand in 1641 to six hundred and sixteen thousand in 1652, much more than half exterminated; and three-fourths of Irish land and five-sixths of Irish houses taken over by British settlers; and, twenty years after Cromwell, three-fourths of the Irish population existing on milk and potatoes, living in cabins without chimney, door, stairs, or window.

Wrote Gookin: "They were strong, they are weak; they were numerous, they are consumed by sword, pestilence and famine; they were hearty, they are out of courage; they were rich, they are poor and beggarly; they had soldiers, they are left naked; they had cities, they have but cottages."

"So," Petty concluded on Cromwell's achievement, "they will never rebel again."

Cromwell: Lyman's presumed ancestor. Geraldine's. Katrina's. And here you are, Edward, seeking the hand of a woman bred of Cromwellian dust, you, whose father, by memory passed on, traces your lineage back to Connacht then and now.

Katrina entered the library and came to him, reached out her hand and stared into his eyes.

"I'm pleased you're here at last," she said. "Mother and Father will meet you alone, and I'll come back when your conversation is over. I love how strong your face looks today."

"I hope it's strong enough," Edward said. "Will you be able to hear what is said?"

"Oh yes, I shall," she said.

He watched her vanish beyond the doorway, stood with book in hand conjuring his own seventeenth-century forebears: more than two centuries gone since the ancestral Daughertys' lands were taken in Donegal, the clan reduced to lowly cottiers tilling the land of others; some of them turning into the plundering rapparees who preferred the pike to the hoe; but, in time, all of them thrust into the barrens of western Connacht like flung dogs.

Whether my people were marked because they had slaughtered English landholders in the bloody rebellion of 1641, or were unslaughtered remnants-in-arms after Cromwell's 1649 conquest, it matters not, for they go into exile by Cromwellian fiat—the transplanting, he called it—to the far western part of Ireland's most desolate province, without houses, adequate clothing, cattle, or farm implements, prohibited from living within five miles of the River Shannon or the sea. Women and children perished in ditches, dead of starvation or eaten by wolves. In their desolation the Irish fed upon dead bodies dug from graves, the survivors condemned to till the earth of Connacht's hellish landscape and discover its essence: ubiquitous rock.

How goes the family lineage?

It hardens.

And how grows the rock's foetus?

With neither tongue, nor brain, nor soul: doomed creature mutilated in the womb, conceived with one foot, webbed arm, vertical eyes, a row of teeth in its belly, suitable for frightening devils, born on a rock so wide the people of Connacht made it the altar of Jesus, worshiped it in Gaelic prayer, lived off its might, starving as they prayed, their priests axed or hanged, their young men and maidens sent to slavery in the Tobacco Islands where they toiled at a level below the Negro bondsmen; the leftover faithful withering by the tens of thousands, living amid a world of rock fences, those man-high sculptures that ride the contours of hills and valleys still, lace-made to foil the wind, an endless, timeless memorializing of rock in order to live free of it: fences visible for miles, miles, and miles beyond that, each rock a gravestone, each fence testament to the ingenuity of survival: leaving, where the rocks were liftable out of the earth, scrubby patches of soil for planting.

The lineage leads from Connacht's fences forward to famine, when even potatoes die, then into modern exile on Connacht Block in Albany, raucous overcrowded neighborhood at Madison Avenue and Quay Street, where greenhorns cluster till they find footing, send money away for others to quit the rock, then move uptown, to the North End like the Daugherty brothers, Owen and Davy first, then Emmett, or they rise like you, Edward Daugherty, to heights where you can court the modern get of an ancient devil.

I am demonizing my love, Edward thought, to make her the equal of what her parents think I am.

He returned the Irish books to their shelves, and he waited. Fletcher brought sherry and three glasses. Edward stared at it: Waterford crystal, brought here by Lyman.

"The Master thought you might like a bit of sherry," said Fletcher, setting one glass apart.

"They *are* going to see me," Edward said.

"They will be along presently," said Fletcher, nodding.

"I've already read all the books."

"You are accomplished at many things, Mr. Daugherty." And Fletcher left the room.

Edward knew what Jacob and Geraldine would say to him, had long absorbed their hostility in the foreshortened glance, the abrupt tone, the bristling at his closeness to Lyman: for that closeness differed in kind from Lyman's behavior toward his children. It was Lyman's duty as an unmurdered man to see that Edward escaped what fate had ordained at birth for his kind. Edward *was* transformed, and Lyman lived to know his godson had grown and flourished, would even publish a novel, though Lyman would not live to hold it in his hand. But what Edward's transformation would win him remains to be seen. Now here he sits, waiting to be judged, and he feels his brain on fire with ancient yearnings for justice and comprehension.

But I will not kiss their foot.

Well enough. Do you know what they'll say to you?

They'll say the disparity between families and religions will cause friction among friends and relatives, be a curse on the marriage. They will never mention the Irish or that they see us as a race of beasts.

They will imply, with exquisite finesse, that you are of lowly financial status, that Katrina stands to inherit great wealth, and that this wealth has given her her life as she knows it. You, a writer, could you, in a lifetime, ever earn enough to preserve her birthright? Not likely.

They will praise you as a cultured man and wish you well in your literary pursuits, but they will continue to believe Katrina's attentions should be from a suitor of an established profession. You, Edward, being no such thing, stand as a living impediment to a harmonious marriage, in Katrina's mind if not in your own.

He poured himself a sherry, bolted it. It tasted like the Irish Sea.

He leaned back in the leather chair, considered his position, moved a straight chair to a point where it would face the two leather chairs. He sat in the straight chair and leaned forward — no, too close — moved the chair back a foot, poured another sherry, bolted it.

They came in together, Geraldine still growing wide with age, wearing a long black dress that covered her from throat to toe and could have passed for a mourning vestment (anticipating the deathlike eventuation of losing Katrina to this man?). Jacob came in with his high white collar and his unruly graying hair, and Edward stood to greet them, blocking Jacob's access to his desk chair.

"You have something to tell us?" Jacob asked.

"I do," Edward said.

The Taylors made no move to sit down.

"Jake, Geraldine, please sit," Edward said. "I have a few things to say, no sense standing."

Geraldine sat in one of the leather armchairs, and Jacob, not taking his eye off Edward, sat warily beside her. Edward reseated himself on the hardback, facing his captive audience.

"I'm here," he said, "to say directly to you that I've asked Katrina repeatedly to marry me, and she has not said no, but neither has she said yes. I know she's indecisive because you have questions and uncertainties about such a marriage, and about me, which is natural."

Jacob moved as if to speak, but Edward pressed on.

"I don't want to trouble either of you to speak of this now. I want only to reveal to you who I am, for even though you think you know me, you truly do not.

"I begin with this room, where the worlds of your family and mine exist side by side on your bookshelves: Dickens and Thackeray, giants in the world I aspire to, alongside chronicles of your exalted ancestral civilization. I'll live my life writing, books now, perhaps plays in the future, a noble profession, playwriting, as you know from Shakespeare on your shelves.

"I'm sure you've heard what the gossips say about Katrina and me, that I'm aiming above my station. I don't answer such gossip and Katrina admires me for it. After all, who's to say what my station is? Am I fresh from the low life of the Dublin slums? Am I a rude peasant late off the stony fields of Connacht? These things may have been part of my ancestry, just as you two derive from a culture of avaricious land barons who kept farmers in unspeakable peonage for two centuries, from generations of soulless men who grew rich off the slave trade. Is that low life, or —"

"What's that about the slave trade?" Jacob asked. "If you're implying —"

"Don't reduce yourself, Jake, don't give it a second thought. I don't," and Edward quickened his speech, eliminated pauses, breathed on the run.

"I know these are old and generic accusations, and I also know how high you've risen above those early scoundrels who populate your ethnic history. Only a fool would hold it against you. What a glorious heritage you have in the Staats family, paragons of religious liberty, vigorous giants of commerce, and yet there *was* old Jacobus Staats who scandalized his townsmen by marrying a squaw, did he not? Yes, he did, and so what? Who cares who marries whom if the bride and groom are blissful?"

Jacob squirmed, his mouth forming a rebuttal, but in his eyes the question: What exactly is this man saying? Edward poured three glasses of sherry as he spoke and, without losing a beat, put two of them in the hands of Jacob and Geraldine, downed his own, and stood and paced before them, a dynamo of pent energy made visible and audible.

"Henry James, the old man—you both know him, he went to Albany Academy before me—argues that Adam's fall from Eden was necessary for Adam to achieve a higher plane of existence. And I mean to tell you that Katrina and I are now together at the gates of our own Eden, and we couldn't be more sure of our happiness.

If a fall is fated I believe we'll rise to that higher plane, just as Adam did. We'll thrive, we'll transcend whatever society tries to do to us. We'll move onto the grand stage and I'll prosper formidably and achieve heights no lawyer or doctor who might court Katrina could ever know; for I have talent and I have energy and both will last me a lifetime.

"I have a name descended from Irish kings who preexist Oliver Cromwell by six centuries, and I fervently believe in the aristocracy of my lost ancestral world. I'm vividly aware also that your ancestors, Geraldine, going back as they do to Cromwell's England, your ancestors, in the name of God, tried to eliminate the entire population of Ireland, and almost succeeded. Then I sit here and all that self-glorifying butchery leaps out at me from the pages of books in this room—clear proof the past is behind us, that we're in a new world with a new light on our own days, and you, Jake, and you, Geraldine, have the strength and courage to keep—*in your own library*—the record of those unspeakable crimes. Hurrah, I say to this. Hurrah for you both, hurrah for facing the worst history has to offer, and moving forward to honorable success in every realm worth inhabiting—civic, business, ecclesiastical, social, but, most of all, success in conceiving and raising the peerless Katrina, icon of beauty and wisdom. And so my congratulations to you both, and don't say anything yet. Just think on my words. Think on me as the husband of your sublime daughter. Consider the uncritical love she and I have for each other, and what a rare thing this is in anyone's life."

Then, as these final words of what Edward would come to call his Manifesto of Love and History hung in the air, he backed quickly away from Jacob and Geraldine (who still stared at him, gripping their sherry), found the library door and opened it, and then he was gone.

KATRINA VISITS THE *ANGEL*
OF THE SEPULCHRE

October 10, 1885

HEADACHES WERE COMING gradually to Katrina, then they became intermittent, and, after two weeks, incessant; and so she took to her bed with valerian drops, the only avenue to sleep. When the sedatives worked she slept day into night, read poetry (especially Baudelaire and Verlaine, who, she had learned in school, were abominable writers to be avoided), read them to tire herself with the pleasure of words, and told her family she was not ill, only full of bodily weariness.

Katrina took her meals from a tray and kept reading, marveling at Baudelaire's misogyny: *I have always been astonished that women are allowed to enter churches. What can they have to do with God?*

God, on the arm of the Episcopal Bishop (very high church), came regularly to dinner at Katrina's home. God ate well, stayed late, and the discourse, while boring, was not without merit: for it reinforced the family conviction that evil resided elsewhere, and that divine providence hovered just above the dining room chandelier.

One night she awoke dreaming of panthers running loose in the forest. Her vantage point from an upper story of her house gave her a full view of the threat, and then one of the panthers was inside the stable. Katrina went downstairs to the kitchen, and as she reached for the butcher knife to defend herself, a blue panther, jaws wide in a snarl, sprang out of the bread box. She sat up in a silent scream, her headache gone. She put on her night-robe, walked down to the kitchen, and opened the bread box. She found the butcher knife, cut a corner of bread, and ate it sitting at the window, staring out at that patch of her garden that was illuminated by streetlamps. She could see the Venus fountain, after Botticelli, that her father had bought in Italy, and, around its base, the yellow and orange leaves that were falling from the trees.

Of course the dream was Edward.

She got up from the window and boiled a kettle of water, then went to the china room and took down the Berlin cup and saucer that had belonged to the King of Holland, and the tea service owned by Oliver Cromwell. She made the tea, put the pot and china on a tray, carried it to the front drawing room. She had no precedent for her behavior, but she believed the rightness of every thought, every impulse that came to her.

She lit four candles in the candelabra her mother said was once owned by the Bonaparte family, and sat down for contemplative midnight tea amid family treasures: the Ismari vase mounted in ormolu, the Washington portrait by Rembrandt Peale; the Wentworth mirror, its border embroidered by Lady Wentworth; the portrait, as handsome widow, of Femmitie Staats, ancestor of her father, and direct descendant of Johannes Staats, who had been born in 1642 into Albany's original settlement.

Femmitie's and the Wentworths' presences were reinforcements of family links to the origins of the city and the nation: American life predicated upon Dutchness without end, Albion evermore. I do believe this house is paradise, Katrina thought. I believe it is a palace of brilliant crystal, softest velvet, golden light, pervasive elegance; and memory overflows with beauty and the holiness of history. I see a proud elevation of spirit and mind in the splendid people of my life. I will lose my birthright to these things if I marry Edward.

She slept and at painless morning took breakfast in the dining room with the family, an occasion of relief for all, the cause noted by Katrina's sister, Adelaide: "She's gotten over her lovesickness."

"That Daugherty is ruining the peace of this family," Jacob Taylor said.

Katrina said nothing and after breakfast gave Cora, the chambermaid, her daily fifteen minutes of tutoring in elocution in Katrina's sitting room.

"Is it true as Miss Adelaide says that you're desperate sick in love with Mr. Daugherty?" Cora asked.

"I'm not such a fool," Katrina said. "I know the difference between my body and my soul. Love is the soul's business. I'm sick because my body seems to want this marvelous man. I would never call it love."

"Oh, Miss Katrina, I think you got it backwards."

"You're an expert on love?"

"I'm commonsensical on it. I loved a boy well and do yet, and it's body and soul, Miss, body and soul."

"You do speak your mind, Cora."

"I wouldn't know what else to do with it, Miss."

Katrina's clearest memory of Cora McNally was of the white stone china cup with the broken handle, a memorable stub of unmanageable clay. It was the day Geraldine Taylor hired Cora for scullery work (from which she swiftly graduated), and cook was giving Cora her first lunch, setting her chair and dishes at a solitary place at the drainboard of the sink: a sandwich of turkey scraps and skin dabbed with cranberry sauce, and tea in that unforgettable stone china cup. Cora came in from the scullery, saw this offering, and said not to cook but to Katrina's mother:

"Mrs. Taylor, on the poorest day of me life in Cashel I never ate a meal on the drain of a sink, and if ever a cup in our house broke its handle, we threw it out."

Geraldine nodded and said quietly to cook:

"Sit Cora at the servants' table and give her a proper cup."

And from then forward the Taylor family and its servants knew who Cora was, as you shall know me, Katrina announced silently to all future obstructionists.

Katrina's dilemma: whether to decide in silence to accept the offer of marriage, suffer all losses privately in advance, and move beyond loss, or allow family and peers to mount the inevitable attacks on such outrageous wedlock. Katrina knew her decision would not be influenced by the views of others. The problem lay in protocol, distortion of which would leave scars.

As the days passed, it began to decide itself. Mother must be allowed to invite the Bishop to lecture Katrina on marrying someone outside the religion. Father must be permitted to agree to finance a tour of the Continent to take Katrina's mind off the papist lout.

Katrina looked at the portrait of Femmitie clutching the red rose of love, her shawl over her left shoulder emphasizing the fullness of her right breast; and in Femmitie's mouth Katrina read the flirtatious curl of a smile, supporting the legend that Femmitie fled her parents' unbearably pious Albany home to marry a seductive Boston confidence man (a Dublin rascal masquerading as an Ulsterman) who made her insanely rich, then was, himself, hanged for murdering a wealthy Presbyterian cleric. These events had been irrelevant to Femmitie's sensuous smile, which survived religion, money, and the gibbet. Wrote B: *Woman cannot distinguish between her soul and her body. She simplifies things, like an animal. A cynic would say it is because she has only a body.* You are not talking about me, Katrina told him.

Katrina decided her resurrection from indecision and reclusion would take place two days hence, and she wrote letters organizing the event, the first to Giles Fitzroy, asking that he take her for an afternoon ride to brighten her pallid complexion, expose her weakened spirit to the restorative of fresh air and sunshine; and the second to Edward, asking that he meet her at one-thirty in Albany Rural Cemetery near the *Angel of the Sepulchre*, the one landmark of whose location everyone was certain.

In her parents' estimation, Edward, despite his long-standing family link through Lyman, was now a figure to be kept as remote from Katrina as possible; but Giles, Katrina's childhood friend, was eternally welcome in this house, his father being the Taylor family physician, his mother Geraldine Taylor's colleague in maintaining standards for Albany's social elite.

"Where shall I take you?" Giles asked when Katrina had settled into his cabriolet (top down), his horse leading them at a sprightly pace up Broadway. Katrina covered her lap and legs with Giles's blanket. It was the time of sublime autumn in Albany, the day bright and warm with sunshine, explosive with the reds and oranges and yellows of the dying leaves.

"We should go to the most beautiful place we know," she said. "The cemetery."

"Oh you are cheerful," Giles said.

"But I'm serious. I want to see where the Staatses and Taylors are buried, and decide should I be buried there."

"What puts you in such a morbid mood?"

"Contemplating death isn't morbid, Giles. It's liberating."

"But why now? You're so young and healthy. Why not think of life instead?"

"But I do. And death is so important to it."

"You're as odd as you are beautiful, Katrina."

They drove past St. Peter's Hospital, where Giles was a medical intern, following his father's career, and past her grandfather's foundry. Without Lyman, Katrina and Edward might never have met, and most certainly would not now be contemplating marriage.

"What do you think of me these days, Giles?"

"I think you're heavenly, a goddess among us. I love being with you."

"Will you be my slave?"

"Gladly."

"Oh that *is* good."

They rode over the small bridge where the Patroon's Creek crossed Broadway, through the tollgate by the sandpits onto the Troy Turnpike; then they turned west up the Loudonville plank road toward the cemetery.

"Do you like Edward Daugherty, Giles?"

"He seems a fine fellow, but he's a few years older than I, so we're not close."

"I'm going to meet him."

"When?"

"This afternoon."

"Aren't you with *me* this afternoon?"

"You're taking me to him."

"Katrina, I don't understand anything about you."

"That's all right, Giles. I understand everything about you and I'm very fond of you."

" 'Fond' is a terrible word."

"A true one."

"Where are you meeting him?"

"At the cemetery. By the *Angel of the Sepulchre.*"

"This is ridiculous. I feel like a fool."

"But aren't you my slave?"

Giles fell silent and they turned and drove along the crest of the hill that was Rensselaer Avenue, past the Fitzgibbon country mansion, where her mother's eccentric brother Ariel dwelled in baronial excess, and where Katrina had never been at ease. When she saw that Giles's silence had become a sullen pout, she reached over and took his hand in hers. By the time they passed through the south gate of Albany Rural Cemetery and were approaching the Angel, his pout had melted into an abashed smile.

"Come back for me at four o'clock," Katrina said as she stepped down from the cabriolet near the statue of the Angel. She folded Giles's blanket over her arm. "I'll take this in case I have to sit somewhere and wait."

"Why are you meeting him?" Giles asked.

"I'm not sure. If I find out I may tell you."

"You know he just writes for the newspaper. He's only a writer."

"I read him with great appreciation for his intelligence. Have you read the novel he just published?"

"I don't bother myself with novels. But I've heard it said he keeps fast company."

"There is none faster than I," Katrina said.

"At that the slave exits," Giles said, urging his horse forward.

A quarter hour early for Edward, Katrina walked to the Angel, who was sitting on the rock he had rolled away from the sepulchre of Jesus, atop the gravestone of the Banks family from Albany. Since his arrival in 1868, this heavenly, white-marble emissary had become the best-known resident of the cemetery, eclipsing magnates and governors, even heroes of the Revolution, and daily drew crowds of the curious and the reverential, although today only two women were standing off, staring at him. The Angel had also enhanced the fame of his creator, Erastus Dow Palmer, neighbor of Katrina's for as long as she had been able to look out the window and see him striding along Elk Street with his walking stick and his great white beard. Instrument of the resurrection, the Palmer Angel, in flowing white nightshirt, hair of Jesus length, folded wings as tall as his seated self, stared out into Katrina's afternoon and thrilled her, bringing her again to the edge of tears with the beauty of his irreality, the perfection of his fingers and toes, the strength and certainty in his mouth and eyes. He was speaking to the known and unknown Marys who had come to weep over the dead Jesus: "Why seek ye the living among the dead?" he asked them.

Sentinel of salvation, rock of redemption, he knew what he was about. No perfection in bedridden indecision, Katrina. The Kingdom of Heaven belongs to the clear of heart; you know that. (Yes, yes, of course. But what, besides clarity, inhabits the heart of an angel?)

"Beauty regards beauty," came Edward's voice, and Katrina turned to see him in his phaeton two-seater, looking so spirited, so ebullient, even sitting still: as fine a figure, she suddenly decided, as she would find this side of the angels. She walked toward him and he took off his hat to greet her and leaped down to take her hand, help her up into the seat beside his own.

"I didn't expect this day," he told her. "Your invitation thrilled me. But how did you get here?"

"I have my slaves," she said.

His dark-brown eyes focused only on her and she thought he owned the handsomest head of brown hair imaginable, and she thought: I'll bet he took off his hat to woo me with his hair.

"Do we have a destination?" he asked.

"Where the road leads," she said, and Edward told his horse to take them along it.

Katrina could navigate all of the cemetery's vast natural beauty, knew each vale, brook, and ravine, knew the cypress grove, the pond by the elm woods. And she knew many of its residents, could identify the replica of Scipio's tomb where Jared Rathbone, Lyman's old friend and business enemy, was buried, and the thirty-six-foot Doric column commemorating Albany's heroic Revolutionary general, Philip Schuyler, and the granite sarcophagus of General

James Rice, once of Elk Street, who, dying at Spotsylvania, said, "Let me die with my face to the foe," and Thurlow Weed, founder of the *Albany Evening Journal*, whose Republican politics her father detested, and the very, very rich William James, whose grandson Henry wrote novels of great convolution that intimidated Katrina, and the banker Billings Learned, Katrina's favorite capitalist, who wrote on his wife's headstone: "Wife, I thank my God upon every remembrance of you."

These notable graves gave comfort to Katrina in her pursuit of love, perhaps marriage. This gilded world of the familiar dead, a world into which she had been born and raised, filled her soul with cultivated joy, for her mother had sensitized her to the splendor of an eminent death, which, as all know, perpetuates an eminent life.

But now the beat of her heart also importuned Katrina, and as they came to a grove of blue spruces, with no monuments or people in sight, she said to Edward, "Stop here. It's all as I remember. No corner of the world more beautiful."

While Edward tethered his horse, Katrina climbed down from the carriage and, with blanket in hand, walked to a shaded place beneath the holy trees, whose wood was one of the principal sources of her father's abundant wealth. The tall spruces had shed needles and cones in a soft carpet upon the earth, and atop this carpet Katrina spread Giles's blanket. She unpinned her hat and set it on the blanket, then sat and looked up at Edward, who was watching her private drama play itself out.

"Come and sit," she said.

"You seem to know exactly what you're doing," Edward said. "This is indeed a secret place."

"I've been thinking about it endlessly, ever since your talk with my parents."

"The hymeneal event," he said. "Does this mean you finally have an answer to my question?" He took off his coat and sat beside her.

"Put your face near mine," she said. "I want to know how I'll react."

Edward moved close and, when their noses almost touched, he smiled.

"Stop smiling," she said.

They studied each other's eyes, mouth, hair. She parted her lips and moved her mouth onto his. She held the kiss, stopped it, withdrew to a distance of inches.

"I like it," she said.

He took the game away from her and kissed her, as he well knew how to, and she folded herself into a condition for which anterior planning could not have prepared her.

"Oh that is *very* good," she said, and she resumed the kiss. When it came to a stillness she stared for a long time at Edward, decisions being made by her eyes and by a pervasive bodily tension that was thrilling.

"It's clear," she said, "that we now have to do the rest. I've worn as few garments as possible."

"The rest?" Edward said.

"I've read all about this," Katrina said. "It's nineteen days since my time. I now have nine days when I cannot conceive. It's an ideal moment for the estrus to strike, and strike it has."

"This is a very bold act, Katrina."

"You don't accept me?"

"I accept with great heart but wild misgiving. We're marked forever if something happens."

"I sense the ecstasy I've heard about. I want to be certain it exists."

"I love you for this, Katrina, more than I loved you yesterday, and I didn't think that possible. You're a wonder."

"You're all the world to me now, Edward. But I must confirm that you are truly real. Do you understand?"

"I don't think I understand why we're establishing my reality in the cemetery."

"We'll die before we get to it if you don't shut up," and she arched her buttocks off the blanket, raised her skirts to her waist, and unbuttoned the top of her dress as Edward fell on his knees in front of her.

"Why seek ye the living among the dead?" the Angel asked Katrina, and her answer came that, in her, there had taken root the truths of her poet: that death is the divine elixir that gives us the heart to follow the endless night, that it is the mystical attic, the poor man's purse, the mocker of kings, the accursed's balm, the certain loss that vitalizes possession. She feared it not at all, and chose to behave as if each moment were the ultimate one; and this consistency, to the end of her days, would astonish all who knew her.

Edward, who had won her eye with his brash flirtation, and now was gaining her virginal body, believed *he* was the privileged one to be given such a sumptuous gift as the mythic ideal that was Katrina. And he told himself: You, Edward Daugherty, you, now prostrate on this exquisite altar, you own a fortunate heart.

After a time that he would remember not by its length but by the intensity of his joy, he felt and heard her approaching her peak, felt it also in himself, and he moved out from her sweet place to spill his seed on the carpet of brown pine needles; for God can be tempted only so far.

"Are you always so cautious with life?" Katrina asked.

"I don't want to lose you, now that I have you," he said.

"Because you did that, did you love me less?"

"Because you court danger," he replied, "do you love me more?"

"You don't understand," Katrina said.

"Perhaps it's you who don't understand."

"We'll marry in the spring, I understand that," she said.

"People are already trying to stop us."

"We'll overcome them."

"Love will prevail over everything."

"We'll live like no other people ever lived."

"Only death will undo us," he said.

"Amen," she said.

Confirmed anew that a voluptuous woman is the universe's greatest gift to a man, Edward turned back to Katrina, bent low and kissed her mouth. Stroking himself then, because this must not end, and seeing and feeling Katrina's blood on his hand, he made his inward thrust, thinking: Do whatever you will, Lord. This is worth it.

EDWARD BRINGS KATRINA
HOME TO MAIN STREET

October 20, 1885

MAIN STREET WAS the second-last street in the North End, one of five block-long streets that sloped down from Broadway to the railroad tracks and the Lumber District. After these streets only a few isolated houses dotted Broadway before the Bull's Head tavern and Island Park racetrack, and then came the open road that ran north toward Troy. Houses stood only on the north side of Main, the south side as wooded with oak and maple and elm as it had been the day Dutchmen first left their boat to set foot on this land of the Mohawks. The five small streets were a community to Edward, a cul-de-sac of rustic, harmonious life, lived adjacent to the chug and clatter of Albany's three lifelines: the rail, the canal, and the river. As he turned the corner in his carriage, Edward saw his mother and the Whites standing in front of the Daugherty house, then saw his father's head halfway out the bedroom window.

"They're talking to neighbors," he said to Katrina, beside him.

"Is that bad? Do you want to come back later?"

"No, neighbors are good. They'll cut the ice. It's Cappy and Mamie White."

"Such a large woman."

"She's larger than that. Cappy drives the Lumber District horse-car and when she gets on the front of it the back end goes up."

"Does she have to be so big?"

"They've had doctors, but she keeps growing. It's been like watching the slow inflation of a balloon for as long as I've known her."

A brown chicken ran into the street as Edward pulled up, and his mother, an apron over her long housedress, ran after it, snatched it up and held it under her arm. Edward reined the horse, and as he jumped down to tether it, Katrina said to him, "That's your mother."

"It certainly is."

"I remember her."

He helped Katrina down from the carriage, then walked her over to introduce her first to his mother, then to the Whites, as his fiancée. His father was gone from the window.

"Katrina says she remembers you," Edward told his mother.

"From the Manor House," Katrina said. "My mother took me to visit the Van Rensselaer girls when I was eight or nine, and when we played in the kitchen, you were there. I remember how young you were, and yet your hair was pure white."

"I do remember your mother came often," Hanorah Daugherty said. She smiled at Katrina. "But I wasn't so young, I don't think."

"Oh, but you were," Katrina said.

"We'll move along, Hanny," Cappy White said. Cappy was a burly six-footer with a thatch of bristle on his upper lip, and already graying at thirty-eight. "Congrats to you, Eddie."

"Thanks, Cappy. I deserve them."

"You have a beautiful, beautiful bride," Mamie White said. She stared at Katrina, then gave Edward the saddest of smiles.

"She's not my bride quite yet, Mamie. But we're getting there."

The Whites said their goodbyes and walked off slowly, Mamie's shoulders rocking from side to side.

"Go on in, go in," Hanorah said, shooing them toward the front door. "I'll put this one back in the yard," and she walked to the rear of the house with the chicken in her arms.

Edward opened the door for Katrina and led her into the parlor with its huge chrome stove, the beaded valances on the windows, the doilies on the arms of the horsehair chairs. A small braided rug in front of the rocking chair was the only covering on the wide pine-board floor.

Edward moved the wicker rocker into the sunlight for Katrina, and took three tintypes off the otherwise bare white mantelpiece: individual studio shots of his father in a suit and derby, his mother in a full-length flowered skirt, white blouse, and black bonnet tied under her chin with a ribbon; and one photo of them sitting together, with little boy Edward on Emmett's lap.

"This is what we no longer look like," he said, handing Katrina the pictures. "I'll be right back."

He went to find his father, bring him out of hiding. Emmett had said he would go to no wedding, nor would he hear any argument aimed at changing his mind. Edward had revealed this fact to Katrina and vowed he'd confront his own parents as he'd confronted hers.

Katrina said her mother thought him "a rude social climber" and was furious at his suggestion that her family had committed violence against the Irish; and her father, baffled by Edward's "babbling about atrocity and slavery," wondered, "What world is that overeducated maniac living in?"

"But what did they say about the marriage?" Edward asked.

"They disapprove but they honor my choice, and they certainly won't stay away from the wedding, as your father threatens to do. My father wouldn't abide anyone but him giving me away, and Mother will insist on buying my dress and shoes and choosing the flowers and decorating the church. She lives for such things."

Decorating the church. Which church?

Emmett was a different problem.

"I'm thinking of marrying Katrina Taylor" was all Edward had said, and Emmett exploded: "Any kin of Jacob Taylor has to be poison . . . that polished fool . . . that felonious rodent . . . a family of pretenders . . . merchants without souls . . . They aspire to nothing but money . . . It's traitorous marrying one of them after what he did to Davy . . . smashed his mind because he pushed for a better wage . . . I dream of seeing them in rags and clogs. No good can come of it, boy, it's a wrong idea."

"It's not an idea, Papa. She and I, we're a matched pair. We've a great love and she's as bright as any woman alive. She's a woman you only dream of knowing."

"Marry your dream, then," Emmett had said. "I'll not witness it."

Edward now climbed the stairs and glanced at the framed tapestry of the Daugherty crest (a leaping stag) hanging on the stairway wall. The Pittsburgh chapter of the molders' union Emmett helped establish gave it as a going-away gift when Emmett left Pittsburgh to come back to Albany. The family name was stitched under the crest in the Irish: *docararch*. Emmett was fond of explaining that it translated as either "unfortunate" or "disobliging," take your pick.

Edward found his father shoeless, in a fresh shirt and his everyday pants, sitting in his bedside rocker, cleaning his fingernails with a six-inch knife. His hair was the color of granite now, and as wild as the mind beneath it.

"So you brought her home," Emmett said.

"She's in the parlor."

"You know what I think about this."

"Nobody could know what to think about Katrina without talking to her. You don't even know what's going on in *my* head."

"I won't argue," Emmett said. He closed the knife, pocketed it, and bent over to pull on a shoe.

"You won't hear me out? You, the one who's always fighting for the right to be heard?"

Emmett leaned back in the rocker and stared at his son. "What is it, then?"

"It's me, it's what I've become," Edward said, and he felt the same energy rising that he'd known in delivering the Manifesto. He could not taunt his father as he'd taunted the Taylors, for the man wouldn't sit for it. So, then, he would neither pace nor gesticulate. He would keep his energy leashed. He sat on the bed and faced Emmett.

"You raised me and Lyman educated me," Edward said, "and now I'm some kind of new being with no known habitat—not North Albany, not Elk Street. Katrina knows this without my saying it. She's as smart as the edge of your knife. She knows exactly who I am and she loves me and wants to marry me. And God knows I want to marry her. I've never felt anything even close to what I feel with her. It's thrilling, Papa, unbelievably thrilling. I'm not marrying her father, and I'm not condoning what he did to Davy. But is this a blood feud that carries on for generations? Do the wars of the father have to be the wars of the son? I wrote *The Mosquito Lovers*, didn't I? You planted that in my head and I'm glad you did, but I've got other things to write. I'm no soldier in the class war. If I'm geared to do anything it's to celebrate the mind and the imagination. Rise in the world with your brain, not your back and your fists — if you can. And I believe I can. And I believe others can as well as me. Where are the minds of *our* people? Why aren't we running the foundries and lumber mills instead of being molders and handlers all our lives? I'm not against radicalism, but I want to get beyond it. I want to leap over the past and live in a world where people aren't always at each other's throats. I know some of our roots are in the hovels of Connacht and we shouldn't forget that. But there was Donegal before Connacht, and before Donegal who can say? Were we ever anything besides tribal warriors? We were bards, weren't we, some of us? And we were architects of the book. And we had the music, as you always said. If they reduced us to breaking rock to stay alive, those other qualities were still in us, and I see them now in myself. They're not new to me but I look in the mirror and I think, 'You're a new being,' and I wonder what to do about that. Do I lose my past by shaping a future? Do I disinherit myself? No matter what you think, I haven't abandoned the struggle. If you'd heard what I told Jake and Geraldine when I asked to marry Katrina, you wouldn't have turned a deaf ear. I probably made lifetime enemies of them. I don't want to fight with you now, Papa, or ever, just as I don't want to give up this woman, who is everything I value. My love for her seems like a primal force, as basic and as strong as what I feel for you and Mama."

Edward stopped talking. He stood and took two hesitant steps toward the door.

"Now that you know this," he said, "can you still tell me to abandon Katrina to satisfy your vengeance against Jake Taylor? If you can, then I think you're wrong, and I don't believe I ever said that to you before, or even thought it. Now I'm going downstairs and talk to Katrina and Mama. I hope you come down and join us."

❊ ❊ ❊

Katrina had left the parlor. Edward found her in the kitchen, sitting at the table, watching Hanorah at the stove stirring something in a frying pan. The kettle was sending up wisps of early steam and the table was set for five, one extra, of course.

"I saw those children grow up and move off," Hanorah was saying. "Twenty-six years I was with them, from when I went in there to wash pots. Then they found out I could cook and I cooked for the Patroon till he died, and for Mrs. Bayard until she died, too. Then they closed the place up. I still cook for some of the family when they stay the month at Saratoga, but mostly I only cook for himself, and for this one, whenever he comes to see us," nodding at Edward as he entered the kitchen.

He walked to Hanorah and looked over her shoulder at the frying pan.

"Bubble and squeak?" he said.

"You don't like it?" Hanorah said.

"I don't like it, I love it with a passion I reserve only for beautiful women like yourself."

"Listen to the mouth, will you?" Hanorah said.

"Bubble and squeak," Edward said to Katrina, "is this cook's way of joining potatoes and cabbage in God's secret recipe. I presume we're having lunch."

"Miss Taylor said you didn't eat."

"Miss Taylor is Katrina."

"I just met her, if you don't mind."

"You set five places. Is Hughie Gahagan joining us?"

"He might."

"Hughie Gahagan is dead," Edward said to Katrina, "but my mother doesn't give up on him. My father brought him home one night for supper and put him to work in the lockhouse. He stayed five years and we buried him out of the parlor. He had nobody else."

"Emmett brought men home for a meal all his life, especially if they were down on their luck," Hanorah said. "He still does it, so I always set an extra place."

Emmett's step on the stairs silenced the conversation.

"There's a boat in the lock," Emmett said as he came into the kitchen. He looked at no one and walked to the kitchen window that gave a view of the canal at the foot of North Street. He stood looking out, his back to those in the room.

"It's a passenger packet," he said.

No one reacted. After a while he said, "Cappy White, he's a hard-luck man."

"He has more than his share of trouble," Hanorah said.

"He lost a thousand dollars' worth of horses in a fire last year. And then Mamie like that."

"Well, she's getting about," Hanorah said. "She walks the block and she does the garden. She sat in the chair this summer in the garden. She leans sideways and pulls the weeds she can reach. Those she can't she tells Cappy to pull. Sometimes he pulls up the flowers."

"Cappy and I raced horses on the canal in the winter," Emmett said, still staring out the window, "and sometimes up at Island Park on a Sunday, when we had the money. We had fast horses them days."

"We have a very fast horse," Katrina said.

Emmett turned slowly around and stared at her.

"This is my father, Emmett Daugherty, Katrina," Edward said. "He sometimes forgets to say hello to people. And this is Katrina Taylor, Papa. I mentioned her to you."

Katrina nodded at Emmett. "Chevalier is his name," she said. "He's a trotter."

Emmett continued to stare at her.

"We're having bubble and squeak," Hanorah said.

"Is it your horse?" Emmett asked.

"No, my father's," she said.

"Unh," Emmett said and he sat at the table across from Katrina and stared out the back door. The brown chicken pushed through the broken screen of the door and stepped into the kitchen.

"That hen is in again," Emmett said.

"Let her be," Hanorah said.

The hen came over to Hanorah and moved in a circle near her, pecking at the hem of her dress.

"It's all right, Biddy," Hanorah said to the hen.

"My mother's pet," Edward said. "A hen that behaves like a cat."

"She's a bloody nuisance," Emmett said.

"She just comes to see me," Hanorah said. "I bought her as a chick last year at the fair. I saw her born in one of them machines and I paid ten cents for her."

The hen beat her puny wings and lofted herself onto a chair and sat on its cushion.

"Now she'll lay an egg on the chair," Emmett said. "For the love of Jesus will you look at that."

"She lays the egg for me," Hanorah said. "She doesn't know anything about Jesus."

The hen sat, adjusted her rump, stared at her audience and spoke to it — *"toook-a-takaawk"* — shook her rump, laid her egg on the cushion, batted her wings anew, and lofted herself back to the floor.

"She came upstairs and laid one in the bed one morning and Emmett rolled over on it," Hanorah said.

"Isn't it good luck, a hen in the house?" Katrina asked.

"There are those who'd argue with that," Hanorah said.

She picked up the hen and carried it out to the yard, then came back and rinsed her hands under the pump by the sink and wiped them dry with her apron. She picked the new egg off the chair and put it in the icebox with the other eggs and took out the butter and put it on the table. She poured boiling water into the teapot, spooned the potatoes and cabbage into a dish, and took warm bread out of the oven and sliced it. She put it all on the table and said, "We're ready."

She and Edward then sat on either side of Katrina, the spirit of Hughie Gahagan separating Edward from his father. Hanorah caught Emmett's eye and he bowed his head and said silent grace. Then Hanorah passed the bread and the bubble and squeak, and they all helped themselves.

"There's talk now of a wedding," Hanorah said.

"There is," said Edward.

"When did you meet?"

"When we were children, or at least Katrina was a child. Then all of a sudden she grew up and I saw her at Cleveland's victory parade, and she looked like this," and he opened his hand to Katrina's face. "I was conquered, or maybe I was victorious, finding what I didn't even know I'd been looking for all my life."

"Did you feel that way, too?" Hanorah asked Katrina.

"I thought him quite perfect," Katrina said. "I've tried to discover ways to improve him, but I've found none at all."

"You may find some. You're still young," Hanorah said.

"I'm almost twenty. Juliet, had she lived, would've been married six years at my age. Perhaps I'm older than I seem."

"Where would the wedding be?" Hanorah asked.

Katrina looked at Edward. He waited for her to answer, but she did not.

"We've made no plans," Edward said. "We wanted to talk to you before we did anything."

"My parents want it to be at the Cathedral Chapel of All Saints," Katrina said.

"That's where the Episcopalians go," Hanorah said.

"Yes. Bishop Sloane is a friend of the family."

"What do you say to that?" Emmett asked Edward.

"I hadn't heard this," said Edward.

"You marry in that church, you're excommunicated," Emmett said, and he turned to Katrina. "Do you know what you're doing to the man, taking him out of his religion?"

"I had no idea," she said.

"We'll find a way to solve it," Edward said.

"Which is your church?" Katrina asked Edward.

"Sacred Heart, here in North Albany."

"Then we'll marry there. Will that solve it?"

"Are you sure about this?"

"You can't marry in the church if you're not Catholic," Emmett said.

"Then I'll become Catholic. How long does it take?"

"You have to take instructions," Edward said. "A few months, maybe?"

"That's fine. I was thinking of a spring wedding anyway, weren't you?"

"Just like that, you become a Catholic?" Emmett said, snapping his fingers.

"I don't believe it matters which language we use when we talk to God. It's possible I'm really a pagan. If so, I shall now be a pagan Catholic."

"What will your parents say?" Hanorah asked.

"They'll be furious."

"You certainly make quick decisions," Emmett said.

"I do what I think I should do, so I can become what I feel I must be."

The Daughertys fell into silence. Edward stared at Katrina, understanding that with a few words she had transformed herself, become as rare to his parents as he already knew her to be, yet he could not have predicted any word she said. Emmett and Hanorah stared at her, rancor gone from Emmett's face, Hanorah a study in bewilderment. What Katrina had done was akin to her action at the cemetery, and Edward now knew she would have this effect on everyone, that the directness of her idiosyncratic behavior was a singular gift. He coveted it, felt the young man's ambition to conquer life with a stroke, as Katrina just had. But he knew he would live a long time before he understood even where to direct such a stroke. Yet, credit where credit is due, Edward: you intuited the rightness of bringing her here unannounced, and for that much you should congratulate yourself. Blind navigation, a maestro's talent, won the battle for today.

The bells for the noon hour rang in the church belfry.

"Those are the bells of Sacred Heart," Edward said.

"It sounds like a requiem," Katrina said.

"No, just the time of day, the noon hour, time for the Angelus."

Katrina framed a question in her eyes.

"A prayer to the Immaculate Conception and the mystery of the Incarnation," Edward said. " 'Behold the handmaid of the Lord. Be it done unto me according to thy word. And the Word was made flesh. And dwelt among us.' "

"It sounds like bells I heard at a neighbor's funeral," Katrina said. "I remember his widow getting out of a carriage in front of St. Peter's church just as the bells began, and, as she stopped to listen, she swooned and fell on the sidewalk. I thought the slow pealing of the bells was very sorrowful, and yet it was the most beautiful sound I'd ever heard. Will they ring that way for our wedding?"

"I'll see that they do," Edward said.

And he remembered Aristotle: as the eyes of a night bird relate to the bright glare of day, so the soul's understanding relates to those things that are the clearest and most knowable of all. Oh, Katrina, most knowable, you speak the dead language of the soul with dazzling fluency.

THE BULL ON THE PORCH

October 16, 1908

FINTAN (CLUBBER) DOOLEY, a butcher living on Van Woert Street in Albany, came forward to reveal his role in the decapitation of a bull the day before the Love Nest killings. This was, he said, a practical joke popularly known as the "Bull-on-the-Porch Joke." The bull's owner, Bucky O'Brien, told an interrogator he was asleep upstairs over his Bull's Head tavern on the Troy Road (where drovers had penned and watered Boston-bound herds of cattle in years past) and did not hear the rifle shots that killed his bull. He was awakened by raucous singing, accompanied by the banging of a dishpan as percussion, but O'Brien judged this a normal happening in the vicinity of his tavern, and he went back to sleep. Dooley said he had banged the dishpan while singing the song "I Want My Mommy" to cover the sound of the rifle shots.

The bull, named Clancy, a long-familiar denizen of the pasture behind the tavern, had only one eye and was known as a peaceful animal. Dooley said Culbert (Cully) Watson, a sometime hotel clerk, known pander, and erstwhile member of the Sheridan Avenue Gang, shot the bull, whereupon Dooley climbed the pasture fence and, with cleaver, handsaw, and knife, and the expertise gained in the slaughterhouses of West Albany, cut off the bull's head and lifted it by the horns over the fence to Watson, who put it in the back of Dooley's wagon. Dooley and Watson then rode down the Troy Road to Albany and left the head on the stoop of the Willett Street home of Dr. Giles Fitzroy. Dooley said he had known Dr. Fitzroy for many years, that the doctor was a noted practical joker, and that, in a bygone year, Dooley had helped the doctor stage the elaborate "Fireman's Wife Joke." Dooley was persuaded by Watson that putting the bull's head on the doctor's porch was a hilarious way of joking the joker. Dooley was unaware that the presence of the head might have other than comic implications.

The whereabouts of Culbert Watson are unknown at this time.

DINNER AT THE DELAVAN
IS INTERRUPTED

December 30, 1894

"EVENING, MR. DAUGHERTY," the hall porter of the Delavan House said to Edward.

"Evening, Frank. Cold as hell out there tonight."

"Back again, Mr. Daugherty," said Willie Walsh, the liveried bellhop.

"Only place to be on a night like this, Willie," Edward said, guiding the golden-haired Katrina to the door of the elevator, her hair swept upward into a brilliant soft bun atop her head, the lynx collar of her coat high around her exposed ears. Toby the dwarf, also in livery, gave the Daughertys a half-bow, and bade them enter his elevator.

"Going up, Mr. Daugherty?"

"Indeed we are, Toby," Edward said.

Toby closed the door of the small wooden cubicle that accommodated himself and four people, no more, and the car moved upward. Edward and Katrina stepped out at the second floor, walked toward the dining room, and were greeted by a plump and pretty housemaid, in black dress and starched white apron, sitting on a chair just inside the cloakroom doorway.

"Why it's Cora," Katrina said.

"Miss Katrina," said the housemaid, standing to greet them. "Mr. Daugherty." She curtsied and smiled. "Don't you both look elegant. Let me take those coats from ye."

"Welcome to them," said Edward.

"Oh it's terrible frigid out, isn't it, sir?"

"Even polar bears are inside tonight," Edward said.

"Is your sister well?" Katrina asked Cora.

"Oh she is, Miss, she's just fine. Your sister and parents and all, they're inside already."

"They all miss you, Cora. And so do I. I have no one to tell my secrets to anymore."

"Them were good times, Miss Katrina. I'll never, never forget them. I miss you all so much, but isn't that just the way it is?"

Katrina kissed Cora on the cheek. Edward pressed a dollar bill into Cora's hand and then took Katrina's arm and walked with her into the dining room. People were eating at all but two of the dozen tables, and in one corner a harpist and violinist were playing "After the Ball," a song Edward loathed and Katrina loved. Edward saw Tom Maginn across the room, dining with two couples, and recognized one of the men as a powerful New York City Assemblyman. Edward caught Maginn's eye, waved. Katrina nodded to Maginn and smiled.

"Maginn," said Edward. "Busy at work."

Edward's dinner guests were already seated at a round table in the far corner. The party numbered six: Edward and Katrina, Jacob and Geraldine, Katrina's sister, Adelaide, and her new husband, Archie Van Slyke, bright young man out of Harvard Law School, now an assistant vice president of the State National Bank, and whose great-grandfather, in collaboration with Jacob Taylor's grandfather, had assembled a pair of family fortunes by confiscating Tory estates after the Revolution.

Dinner would begin with oysters, be followed with choices of foie gras, shad with sorrel, partridge and cabbage, tenderloin of beef, lobster gratiné (a Katrina favorite), an array of wines, fruit, and cheeses, charlotte russe and Roman punch, Napoleon brandy and Spanish coffee. The menu was chosen by Edward to please the palate of Jacob Taylor, who believed the Delavan served the best food in Albany.

"Can you read your father's mood at this stage of the evening?" Edward whispered to Katrina as they neared their table.

"He doesn't see how this dinner can do anything to stop him from loathing the sight of you," Katrina said.

"I hope to reverse his expectations," Edward said, and with smiles and formality he greeted Jacob and the others, kissing the hands of his female in-laws.

He had ordered small bunches of violets to be at the place settings of the women, and when they arrived Katrina picked hers up and pinned them as a corsage to the breast of her gown. "Flowers, like love," she whispered to Edward, "should lie easy on one's bosom."

Her mother pushed the violets to the center of the table, disowning them. Adelaide sniffed hers, threw Edward a kiss.

"How thoughtful you are," she said.

Of the Taylors, only Adelaide had no censure for Edward; for she had coveted him when he was courting her sister. "If you don't marry him," Adelaide told Katrina when she was abed with indecision, "you're a fool."

Edward had reserved this table in the Delavan's second-floor dining room, which was decorated with sketches and photographs of the luminaries whose visits gave credence to the Delavan's boast that it was one of the nation's greatest hotels. Here was Abraham Lincoln, who supped here before and after he became president, and Jenny Lind, when the hotel was a temperance bulwark, and P. T. Barnum, Oscar Wilde, Boss Tweed and a generation of his plundering ilk, who had made the Delavan a political mecca. Here were actors Edwin Booth and James O'Neill, Albany's Irish tenor Fritz Emmett, the dancers Magdalena Colón (La Última) and Maud Fallon, the actresses Mrs. Drew and Charlotte Cushman, plus one actress who inhabited the American demimonde, photographed in a gown revealing all of her right breast except the nipple, and whom Edward once glimpsed in the Delavan bar, coquettishly urging a swinish, kneeling pol to swill champagne from her slipper.

On this penultimate night of 1894 the hotel was in its political but not yet swinish mode, abuzz with the noise, money, and power of the politicians who had come to Albany for the legislative session that would begin on New Year's Day. The ritual was familiar to Edward, who had dined here often during the years he covered politics for *The Argus*. The festive air, he decided, would be a useful distraction from the heavy mood of this dinner party. The opposing political forces were already feasting and roistering in the two grand suites at opposite ends of the second floor when oysters on the half shell were served to Edward's table.

The maître d' and two liveried Negro footmen approached carrying a box almost the size of themselves.

"Would you give that to the elegant lady over there?" Edward said, and the bellboys set the box on its end beside Geraldine.

"What might this be?" she asked.

"You could open it and find out," Edward said.

"Is this some sort of joke?"

"I assure you it isn't."

"Shall I help you unwrap it, Madame?" the maître d' asked.

"If I must, then please do," Geraldine said.

The maître d' cut the twine that bound the box, then gently ripped away its festive holiday wrapping.

"Open it, Mother," Katrina said.

"Are you in on this?" Geraldine asked. But Katrina only smiled.

"I'll open it," said Adelaide, and she revealed an ankle-length black sealskin coat with high collar and abundant cuffs.

"Gorgeous, it's gorgeous," said Adelaide. "Full-length."

"It's a coat," said Geraldine.

"I'd be abashed if it wasn't," said Edward.

"But what is it for?"

"For you, my dear, for you," Edward said, "a belated Christmas from your daughter and me. You know how things were at Christmas."

Adelaide lifted the coat out of the box.

"I'll try it on for you, Mother," she said, and she slipped into it, with Edward's help, and twirled about so all could see the coat's glory from every angle. "It feels divine," Adelaide said.

Edward noted that the room's other diners regarded the display with smirks and smiles, disdaining the ostentation, admiring the exquisite garment.

"I suppose you want one now," Archie said to Adelaide.

"I wouldn't say no if you brought one home."

"I can't accept this," Geraldine said.

"Of course you can," Katrina said.

"It's too much."

"Not for you," said Edward.

Adelaide took the coat off and held it for her mother.

"Must I?" Geraldine asked.

Then, without standing up, and offering a small smile, she thrust her left arm, then her right, into the sleeves of the coat. Edward could see Jacob relax, not quite into a grin, but that enduring owlish frown of his was fading.

"Very becoming, Gerry," said Jacob.

"It feels so silky," Geraldine said, rubbing the fur with her palms. She took the coat off and folded it into its box. "It's a lovely gift," she said to Katrina.

"It was all Edward's idea," Katrina said.

"Yes. Well, then. Thank you, Edward."

"My pleasure totally," Edward said, snapping his fingers to the maître d', who came forward with a much smaller package and handed it to Jacob.

"Another gift?" Jacob said, squinting at Edward. "Wise men say that gifts make slaves like a whip makes a cur."

"Or a horse," said Edward as Jacob undid the gift wrapping, revealing a pen-and-ink sketch of a racehorse pulling a sulky and driver.

"Very pleasant," said Jacob. "I didn't know this was a night for gifts."

"The picture isn't the gift," Edward said. "The horse is. It's Gallant Warrior. I know how you value a good trotter, and I know how you felt when you lost Chevalier."

"You bought me a horse?"

"He's in Baltimore," said Edward. "And he's yours. We can have him brought up now, or wait for the spring meeting at Island Park, whatever you prefer. He's a handsome animal, and a winner if there ever was one."

"Gallant Warrior is a very classy animal, Jake," Archie said. "He did very well on the circuit this year. He ran second in the Kentucky Futurity."

"Where did you get the money?" Jacob asked Edward.

"You'd be surprised how much novels and plays earn when people like them."

"Which play?"

"Several. Does it matter?"

Jacob smirked, then looked again at the sketch. "You bought me a horse," he said.

From the inside pocket of his coat Edward took a fold of papers and set them in front of Jacob.

"The bloodline, and the ownership papers in your name."

"This is astounding," said Jacob. "Gallant Warrior. He must have cost you a fortune."

"What good is money if you don't spend it on something of value?" said Edward, and he raised his wineglass. "And now, may I wish a joyful holiday to all here, with the sincere hope that harmony settles on our lives in the new year."

The others answered his toast, amid small smiles and waning tension. Katrina surreptitiously patted her husband's hand.

"I must add," said Edward, "that the last play I wrote will earn neither me nor my producers any more money. When its run ends next month in Philadelphia, I'm withdrawing it from performance forever. You probably know which play I'm talking about." He stared at Jacob Taylor.

"You're a clever fellow, Daugherty," Jacob said. "A very clever fellow."

"So they tell me," Edward said.

The play was Edward's latest work, *The Baron of Ten Broeck Street*, a satiric social comedy about a wealthy lumber baron (very like Jacob Taylor) that had earned Edward considerable money and a notable increment of theatrical fame. It owed its existence to Edward's quest to balance his bias; for his previous play, *The Stolen Cushion*, had satirized Albany's lofty Irish bourgeoisie as they were reduced socially by an influx of crude Irish immigrants. Those Irish vied with the Negroes for the nadir of American social status, and, some thought, won. In the play Edward mocked social rising based solely on money. His private quest, he told himself, was to raise the Irish to the intellectual level of nativist Americans, prove the educability of greenhorn multitudes, as he had proven his own, and show those same multitudes how to transcend the peasant caste into which they'd been born.

Instead, the *Cushion* brought down on his crown not only the wrath of the acquisitive Irish, which he had expected, but also the hostility of his father.

"Who isn't looking for a better life?" said Emmett, who had never forgiven Dickens ("that arrogant beggar") for his scurrilous portrait of Irish peasants near Albany in 1842, a year when Emmett himself was struggling upward from the shame of being least; and he now found it necessary, half a century later, to scold his son for the similar dishonor the *Cushion* represented.

Edward had written the *Baron* in part because of Katrina's estrangement from her father, not only for her marriage, but for converting to the Roman Catholic faith. Despite the family hostility, Katrina clove to Edward with fierce loyalty, and married him in Sacred Heart church. Her father endured the formalities of the wedding and gave Katrina away, but as the meaning of her decision pressed in on him he grew more hostile and distant. Because of this, writing a satire on Jacob Taylor's image had seemed to Edward not only apt, but safe. But when the play appeared to resounding huzzahs, first in Albany, then New York and Boston, Katrina quixotically reembraced not only her father, but also the lush comforts of the house on Elk Street, where he had raised her with nannies and servants; and she now yearned for this house in ways Edward judged to be nearly irrational.

Withdrawing the *Baron* from performance was a small loss, a stroke that Edward hoped would render all Taylors respectful of his apparently selfless ways. But in fact he was done with satire and social tracts that aim to reform scoundrels and pave the way to proletarian heaven. Changing the world is elevating work, but better if he could dramatize the mind of Katrina, that complex creature who so dominated his life.

He looked at her sitting beside him, in awe, as always, of her gifts: that serene beauty which masked such lambent passion, those prismatic charms that had taken root in his soul and made him her slave: as a whip makes a cur.

"Are you enjoying your dinner, Katrina?" he asked her.

"You were quite brilliant, my love," she said softly. "You did it all with such panache."

I did it all for the venal streak at the bottom of your elegant heart, he said silently; for his capitulation to Jacob Taylor was, above all, his recognition that unless he acted swiftly, his marriage would bleed to death from Katrina's imagined wounds. He had built their house on a Colonie Street plot next to the Christian Brothers school he had attended. Jack McCall touted him to availability of the land and also built his own home on the same street.

Colonie was an Irish street in the erstwhile aristocratic neighborhood of Arbor Hill, where many of Albany's lumber barons lived. Edward built the house for Katrina as a scaled-down replica of the Taylors' Gothic Revival town house, and, to assuage her loss of the resplendencies she had left behind, he was now refurnishing the interior of the Colonie Street replica in that halcyon Elk Street image—crystal, engravings, chairs, fabrics, lamps—all in the Taylor mode, so that she might simulate her past whenever her fits of neurasthenic nostalgia descended.

While the remodeling proceeded, Edward, Katrina, and their seven-year-old son, Martin, were staying on Main Street with Emmett, who was alone there since Hanorah's death in the spring of '94.

Since the *Baron*'s first production, in spite of Edward's elaborate efforts to comfort her, Katrina had lapsed into prolonged silences, offered him vacant stares and listless, infrequent sex. Edward at first perceived these as her quirkish reaction to his play, but came to believe in a deeper cause: her vengeance against him for luring her away from her maidenly joys with his eloquent tongue, his hot love.

Now his resentment was growing: a muffled fury accumulating toward his wife of eight years. He was stifling it at this instant, admiring the assertive swatch of color the corsage of violets made on her breast, when the waiter served the lobster gratiné. For no reason except his strange intuition to monitor portent, Edward then took his watch from his waistcoat pocket and noted the hour, eight forty-one o'clock, and that Toby, the elevator operator, was waddling, at the highest speed his stubbiness allowed, across the dining room to the maître d'. Edward saw Toby whisper a message, and then return on the run to the hallway, from which Edward now saw smoke entering the dining room.

"Ladies and gentlemen," the maître d' announced in a loud but thoroughly courteous voice, "I suggest that everyone leave with all swiftness. The hotel is on fire."

Edward grabbed Katrina and Adelaide by the arm and moved rapidly away from their table toward the rushing and already whimpering throng that formed an instant clot in the dining room's double doorway. Edward saw the maître d' and Maginn already in the hallway beyond the clot, turned to see Jacob and Geraldine just behind him, and then he rammed himself into the edge of the clot, his force breaking the impasse and sending people stumbling into the hallway toward the stairwells.

In the hall Edward heard Archie behind him saying, with a voice full of panic, "The stairway's jammed and the hallway's full of smoke. We should go to the roof."

"The roof?" Edward said. "How will you get down? Look, this hallway has two staircases."

"The elevator," Geraldine said with a high-pitched gasping that wanted to be a screech, "where is the elevator?"

"Hunker down, get under the smoke if you can, and follow me," said Edward, and the family did as he said and followed him in a crouch along the hall. Edward heard Toby calling, "Here, here, the elevator, I can take one more!" and Edward grabbed Geraldine's shoulder and thrust her at Toby, who pulled her inside the crowded car, slammed the door, and descended to the street level in a rush.

"Mother's coat," said Adelaide, and she ran back to the dining room before Archie could grab her, and vanished in the hallway's thickening smoke.

"Don't die for a coat," Edward yelled to her.

"The roof," said Archie in a voice broken with panic, "we've got to get to the roof! The firemen will get us down."

"You don't even know how to get to the roof," Edward said, but Archie was already on the run into the dining room, pursuing Adelaide.

Two people came toward Edward on their hands and knees, coughing, crying in their fear and asphyxia, a woman in a blue

gown and a man Edward recognized as the New York Assemblyman who had been at Maginn's table. He was dragging a trunk as
he crawled, and when he reached the staircase he pushed the trunk
down the steps ahead of him.

"Come on, Edna," he called to the woman in blue. But Edna had
stopped moving, and Edward saw Jacob wheezing badly, immobi-
lized by the smoke.

"His heart," said Katrina, and Edward lifted Jacob and dragged
him toward the narrow southern stairway. Through the thinning
smoke Edward saw that the New York politician had gotten ahead
of his trunk and was pulling it down the stairs behind him, obliv-
ious of the loss of Edna.

Edward began to cough, and Katrina, who could not stop coughing, fell on the stairs. "We're in hell," she said.

"Only on the outskirts," Edward said. "Don't panic on me. Hold
my coattail so I know you're here." He saw the winding stairway
below, pocked with flame.

"We'll go," he said, but Katrina's cough revealed her weakening
strength, and Edward took off his jacket and wrapped her head
with it. "Breathe through the cloth," he said, "and wait one second," and he crawled back toward the collapsed woman.

"Let's go, Edna," he said, and he dragged her by one arm to the
stairway. Behind him the hallway's carpet in front of the elevator was
a running pathway of flame. No one else would get through that.

"Grab her other arm," Edward told Katrina, and together they
moved down the stairs, Edward holding his father-in-law under his
left arm like a sack of grain, Jacob's head forward, and he and
Katrina pulling Edna, faceup, by her arms. The smoke lessened
dramatically, for reasons Edward could not understand, as they descended to the first-floor landing. They moved down the final flight
to the ground floor, the fire erratically licking only two walls, and
when they reached the billiard room they found four sawhorses
blocking the nearest street doorway, which had been painted earlier
in the day. Edna's husband was throwing his weight against the
door with no success. Edward left the women and Jacob near the
door, picked up the man's trunk and used it as a battering ram,
smashing the door outward and letting in a rush of cold air. He
tossed the trunk out onto the sidewalk and its latch snapped open,

revealing a score of wrapped packages of cash lying atop folded shirts.

He turned back to the women, saw that both were safe from flame, Edna regaining her wits. He went toward them and lifted the now-unconscious Jacob over his shoulder just as Katrina bent down to help Edna rise. Edward then heard a great whooshing sound and in the same instant saw the elevator shaft fill with a sudden rocketlike uprush of flame and gas, a blazing cylinder made visible as the elevator door exploded outward, showering sparks and embers on all in the room, setting fires on the green felt of the pool tables, and hurling into the air blazing splinters and sticks, one of which pierced the breast of Katrina and instantly set her gown aflame. She screamed, bewildered by the wound as she looked at it, and Edward could see the flame blackening petals of her violets. With his left hand he pulled the burning stick from her breast and hugged her to his chest to quench the flaming corsage.

As Edna and her Assemblyman ran to the street, frantically brushing sparks from their hair, Edward moved through the doorway, clutching Katrina ever more tightly with his left arm, the inert Jacob doubled over his right shoulder, a family fusion of three bodies inching toward the outer darkness of the frigid world.

KATRINA VISITS THE RUINS

January 1895

ON THE SECOND day after the fire, despite the pain in her violated breast, Katrina dressed in her winter bloomers and long woolen stockings, two of her warmest sweaters, woolen muffler, heaviest skirt and cape, skating cap that covered her ears, and she rode the trolley downtown. On this cold and sunny morning she left the car and walked to the corner of Steuben Street and Broadway and joined the crowd of a thousand who were watching firemen with hoses wet down the smoldering bricks of the Delavan's ruins so that the search for the missing bodies could begin. She watched people pick up a brick or a piece of pipe as souvenirs, watched three workers trying to pull down a standing wall so it wouldn't topple on the firemen. One worker threw a rope, with a hook at the end, over the wall and, with his mates, then tried to pull the wall down. They tried half a dozen times, but the wall stood. A man in the crowd told the worker with the hook, "Tie a noose around the end of that rope and hang yourself, you dumb mick."

A fireman passed by and Katrina asked him, "Aren't you going to dig for the bodies?" The missing, estimated at a dozen, were all hotel workers. Cora. Her sister Eileen.

"Not today, ma'am. Still got some fire under there, and in some places maybe eight inches of ice on top of that."

Workers would need a month to move ten thousand cubic feet of stone and brick to recover all the dead.

Katrina stared up at where the third floor had been, only the brick facade standing now. On the night of the fire the firemen's hoses wouldn't reach that high, their streams turning into broken plumes just above the second floor and coating the hotel's lower exterior with the glitter of instant ice, a scandal: low water pressure in the city, pressure turned off at night in the antiquated pumping station, and for twenty minutes after the fire started, nobody there to turn it back on.

In two third-floor windows, when they were still windows, when there was still a third floor, Adelaide and Archie Van Slyke appeared in Katrina's memory, Adelaide wearing her mother's sealskin coat. She climbed out and sat on the window ledge to escape the smoke pursuing her. She said nothing, but Archie was cajoling her to be calm while he uncoiled a rope fire escape, a single braid, and fed it out the window and down toward Broadway, where his in-laws, and a crowd that would grow to twenty thousand, watched. Firemen inched the great weight of their ladder along the icy wall to a point beneath the imperiled Van Slykes, and two firemen began the upward climb. It was suddenly clear that the ladder would not reach the third floor (four stories up), clear also that Archie's escape rope (designed for a room two floors down) did not even reach the top of the ladder.

Jacob Taylor said then, "They're as good as dead." He was lying propped in the doorway of Iligan the Bootmaker's shoe repair shop across from the hotel, awaiting a carriage to take him to St. Peter's Hospital.

"They'll get them," Edward said to him, and Katrina ripped her petticoat to make a bandage for Edward's blistered left hand.

As the flames rose up wildly behind her, Adelaide chose to make her silent leap. She clutched the sealskin coat around her and, to the shrieks of the crowd, pushed herself feet-first toward the firemen on the ladder, swiping both men with her leg (neither man lost his grip on the ladder), bounced onto the trammeled snow cushion of Broadway's sidewalk, and landed at the feet of the half-dozen firemen holding the ladder.

"She's dead," Katrina said, and she wailed like a wounded hound and buried her head in Edward's embrace.

Then Edward saw Adelaide stand up and talk to the firemen. "She's *not* dead," he said. "Look at her, she's up."

Katrina looked and saw Adelaide, then kissed Edward.

"God help her live," Jacob Taylor said.

The firemen on the ladder reached upward toward Archie, who now dangled from the end of the rope just above the second-floor window. A chorus of voices in the crowd yelled to him, "Hold on . . . they've nearly got you . . . don't let go." The topmost fireman's hands reached Archie's shoes, then touched them (to a cheer, Katrina remembered), then gripped them both, and at that moment Archie let go of the rope and let himself fall palms-forward to meet the hotel wall. The second fireman grabbed his pantleg and then his knees, and together the two firemen eased him down atop their backs and shoulders onto the ladder. The crowd sent up its roar.

When Katrina learned there would be no digging for bodies today, she took the trolley back to North Albany.

Edward explained to Katrina how it was possible that a flaming stick could fly through the air and pierce her breast.

A porter emptying ashes from the furnace, he told her, had spilled embers on a pile of rags in the basement, without knowing what he'd done. Allowed to kindle unseen, the smoldering rags became the cellar fire that sent foul smoke, and eventually sparks, up the stairwells and heating vents, igniting the south wall of the staircase, and creeping along that wall to the elevator shaft.

The shaft's four wooden walls glistened with spattered oil, Edward said. The wooden elevator cab was built to glide on its cables three inches away from all walls, making the shaft a perfect chimney with perfect draft. The fire licked that oily interior but once, and then blew skyward with instantaneously-cubed ignition that shaped the shaft as a fiery skyrocket, as perfect in its elemental power as the stack of a blast furnace. It swiftly turned the elevator cab into a blazing coffin, and then shot fire through the roof, exploding disaster onto the attic superstructure. The ravenous blaze trapped a dozen employees in their windowless bedrooms under the attic eaves, the only exit door to the roof nailed shut by management to keep housemaids and kitchen boys from loafing, from watching parades pass by on Broadway, to keep them from sleeping on the roof on those summer nights when temperatures in the attic hit a hundred and five. The door burned to ashes, and there was no proof of the nailing. But surely, Edward said, those trapped people must have tried to reach the roof to save themselves, for the hotel had no fire escapes, no fire axes, no hand grenades, no standpipes; and the fire extinguishers hadn't been examined for eighteen months, and many did not work.

Not a dozen but fourteen people lost. Cora and Eileen.

The stack of a blast furnace.

You can see how it could blow a stick through the air to stab you, Edward said.

Geraldine Taylor, recounting her escape for her family, said she had moved through the main lobby, coatless in the early exodus, and out onto Steuben Street, where firemen pointed her toward the Dutch Kitchen, an all-night lunchroom that had become one of several havens for the dispossessed and the injured. She stood in the zero-degree night, searching the thousands of faces, watching the hotel entrance for a glimpse of her family, until she could no longer bear the cold, then went to the lunchroom, which was already out of all food except bread and coffee. Two doors away, in the sheltered doorway of the bootmaker's shop, Jacob Taylor would soon lie in the care of his daughter and Edward.

Geraldine would not see Alelaide's leap, or Archie's rescue, would not see Jacob lifted into the same carriage with Adelaide and Katrina, to be taken together to the hospital. She heard from Maginn, that vulgar reporter, that all were alive but injured, and had gone to St. Peter's Hospital.

"And Edward is still looking for you, Mrs. Taylor, searching the crowds," Maginn said. "They don't know whether you're alive or dead."

Geraldine did not wait to be found by Edward. She walked the eleven blocks to the hospital without a coat and caught such a cold that Dr. Fitzroy thought it might turn into pneumonia; and so kept her home in bed for a week.

Adelaide was hospitalized, and in three days, willful woman, walked out of the hospital without help. Three days after that, she developed such pain that Dr. Fitzroy readmitted her, fearing for her life.

Katrina was a presence in the ruins, whatever the weather; two hours a day, or more, watching the work crew grow from six to sixty, coming to know the foreman, the fire chief, the coroner, the policemen, watching ice hacked and shoveled off the debris as the January thaw arrived, hydraulic mining having failed to loosen the debris: for the stream from the hose was too weak. Relatives of the missing sought out Katrina, confided in her; and she locked in memory the names of the fourteen: Florence Hill, housekeeper; Anna Reilly and Mary Sullivan, linen-room workers; Ellen Kiley, laundress; Thomas Cannon, sweeper; Toby Pender, elevator man; Ferdinand Buletti, cook; Nugenta Staurena, vegetable cook; Bridget Fitzsimmons, kitchen girl; Simon Myers, coffee boy; Molly Curry, Sally Egan, and Cora and Eileen McNally, chambermaids.

Tom Maginn of *The Argus*, Edward's bohemian friend, crossed the street toward Katrina. She'd met Maginn before she became involved with Edward, met him skating on the canal when she was nineteen, a flirtatious afternoon. He was tall, had a bit of a shuffling walk, a mustache now that grew long and drooped, a strong jawline, some might say. At their first meeting he said he knew who she was, "the yellow-haired princess of Elk Street," and he confessed he could never court her, for he had no money, no prospect of any.

"You are the most sublime woman I've ever met," he had told her, "but I'm below your class. I'm a slug in the cellar of your palace."

She had not spoken to him again until he came to the wedding rehearsal as Edward's best man. Edward had asked his father to be best man, but Emmett said he would not stand on any altar in front of God with Jacob Taylor.

Now, hands in his pockets, Maginn tipped his hat, smiled.

"The city is talking about you," he said. "My editor wants me to write about why you come to the ruins every day."

"I want to bury the dead."

"Which dead?"

"The McNally girls. Cora was our housemaid until her sister came from Ireland, and they got a job together."

"You're here because of a housemaid?"

"Cora was very special. We told each other things."

"Did she tell you she was married?"

"Cora?"

"I talked with her husband. He was a pastry chef at the Delavan, but was let go. They married secretly a month ago to bind themselves together, no matter what happened."

"Oh, the poor man, he must be devastated."

"I told him I'd let him know when they find her. What about yourself? I heard you were seriously burned."

"It's nothing compared to what others suffered. And you? We saw you at dinner. Were you hurt?"

"Not a scratch, not a singe."

"You were fortunate."

"Yes, and your husband, he's one of the heroes of the fire. He always seems to rise to the occasion."

"He saved my father's life. And my mother's. And that poor woman from New York."

"You helped save that woman, too. You needn't be modest."

"I did what Edward told me to do," Katrina said.

"Anything I can do for you? The slug, as always, is at your service. You only have to ask."

"I can think of nothing to ask. Please don't write anything about me."

"It wouldn't embarrass you, I assure you."

"Any story would embarrass me. Please don't. This is what I ask you."

"All right, Mrs. Daugherty," Maginn said, and with a smile added, "Now you owe me one."

At dusk this day the workers found the first body. Until then the chief discovery had been the safe owned by Ozzie Parker, who ran the cigar stand in the lobby. The safe had protected Parker's ledgers, gold and silver coins, and seven boxes of cigars, still unlit. The found body was a legless torso, head and one arm attached, sitting erect. It was Mrs. Hill, the housekeeper, identified by her protruding teeth; and under her arm an album of tintypes, all defaced by the heat, no one recognizable.

As the light of day faded, a dozen lanterns surrounded the dig with ceremonial light, and families of the dead moved closer to the ruins, Katrina in the vanguard. One worker with a spade brought up a blue worsted vest. When he held it up to the light of two lanterns, a man came out of the crowd and said, "That's Simon Myers's vest."

"How might you know that?" the foreman asked him.

"I gave it to him," the man said. "He's my son."

"I'm sorry for that, Mr. Myers, but we won't be digging him up tonight."

"Why not, in heaven's name?"

"Just too dark. These men been here eleven hours, and I hate to say this, but the smell up from there is tough to work in. We'll let the grave here air out and get back at it in the mornin'."

Most workers were smoking pipes to mask the odor of the malignant vapor that rose from the ruins. To Katrina the odor had been an onset of reality, a proof that death was more than an assumption. Workers put the lanterns in a circle around the open grave and the coroner ordered police to guard the dig. Twice during the night they chased away a bulldog.

On the next morning at half after midnight, the seventh day after the fire, Adelaide died in the hospital. Katrina and Geraldine were with her. Jacob, on the floor above, was unaware she'd been readmitted, for Dr. Fitzroy cautioned against shocking him. He would sedate Jacob when it came time to tell him his daughter died of a ruptured spleen, suffered in her leap from the window. Edward brought the carriage to take Katrina and her mother home. Katrina put her mother to bed and told Edward she would stay the night at Elk Street.

She lay on the canopy bed in Adelaide's old room, a room of memory now: her old hobbyhorse, and the dozen and a half dolls of all nations, a new one every Christmas, and the Phrygian cap of liberty that was a gift from the French Ambassador when he came to the Taylor home for a dinner in his honor (the cap was supposed to be Katrina's but was handed to Adelaide by mistake), and the Cleveland for President poster, and the toy sailboat, differing only in color from Katrina's, that the sisters had sailed together on Washington Park Lake.

Katrina, incapable of sleep, imagined how she might have diverted the course of life from the dreadful conclusion it had come to this night: by not letting Adelaide run away from them at the fire, by not siding with her parents against Edward, by not yielding to Edward's plan to win back their goodwill with his dinner and gifts. By not marrying him.

She told her mother's servants to monitor Geraldine, make her breakfast, keep her in bed through the morning. Then she dressed, ate freshly baked bread with butter and coffee, and walked down Elk Street, past the city high school, and down Columbia Street to the Kenmore Hotel, where she bought an *Argus* at the hotel's cigar stand. The paper reported there would be a Catholic mass for the dead at St. Mary's Catholic church. Eleven of the dead were Catholic, three Protestant. Protestant ministers and mourners would be welcomed. When all bodies were presumed recovered they would be buried in a mass grave at St. Agnes Catholic Cemetery unless relatives claimed the remains. But who could say whose remains were whose?

Toby Pender might have been buried in an unmarked grave had not Edward bought not only a grave but a sculpted sword-bearing granite angel to mark the resting place of the fire's principal hero, the man who saved Geraldine, among many, and who deserved more than anonymity in death. When he first discovered the smoke, Toby rode his cab to every floor to alert all in earshot, picked up passengers, returned for stragglers, returned again, and yet again on a fourth trip, and was rescuing a lone woman guest when the blast of fire incinerated them both. Toby's and the woman's presences were verified four weeks later, in the final stages of the dig, days after the mass burial, when the woman's melted diamond ring and Toby's tiny crooked spine were found at the bottom of the shaft, along with fleshless, disheveled bones that crumbled at the touch.

Katrina left the Kenmore and walked down to Broadway and stood at her post by the ruins. She was there ten minutes before the digging resumed at eight o'clock. By ten-thirty parts of eight bodies had been resurrected: part of a thighbone and a pelvic bone, both looking like coal; a wristbone with crisp flesh; the cloth of two dresses, one brown, one black with a weave of dark blue on the skirt's hem, both fragments of cloth found adhering to the same flesh.

"It looks to us that these two died in each other's arms," said the coroner to a group of reporters, Maginn among them. "We guess they were under the bed, and fell through to the kitchen, where the fire was hottest. The kitchen and bakeshop were both full of grease and just fed the fire."

"Those dresses may have belonged to the McNally sisters," Maginn said to the coroner. "Her husband here recognizes the design in the black one."

Katrina approached Maginn and Cora's husband. She stared at the husband, who was holding the piece of dress and weeping. She touched the man's arm.

"I knew Cora very well," she said. "Please let me help you bury her and her sister."

The husband looked at this stranger, then at Maginn.

"This is Mrs. Daugherty," Maginn told him.

"We can't help whom it is we love," Katrina said to the man. "We must learn to avoid love. Love is a mask of death, you know."

"What's that?" asked the husband.

"Death is venerable. You can always count on death." Katrina began to weep, dabbed her eyes with a handkerchief, saw Edward pushing through the crowd toward her.

"Forgive me," she said to Cora's husband. "I weep all the time lately. I weep for everybody. It's a pity what people come to be."

"What's going on?" Edward asked.

"I think you should take her home," Maginn said.

"Yes," said Katrina. "There's other death at home, isn't there, Edward?"

"Yes, there is, my dear," Edward said. "I know how you love death, how you need it," and Katrina smiled at him and wept anew. Maginn and Cora's husband could only stare at the two of them.

In a subsequent diary entry Katrina fixed on the fire as the point of transformation of Edward's and her lives into a unity that transcended marriage, love, and a son:

> We were united through the fire in freakish fusion, like Siamese twins with a common heart that damned us both to an intimacy that not only *knew* the other's every breath, but knew the difference between that every-breath and the signal breath that precedes decision, or unbearable memory, or sudden death. We now live out an everlastingly mutual curse: "May the breath of your enemy be your own."

Two months after the fire, in the unbanishable melancholia that followed the death of his daughter, Jacob Taylor died of a massive heart attack. Katrina was not the one to articulate the accusation, but she came to believe what her mother had said first: Edward killed Adelaide and Jacob.

KATRINA AT EMMETT'S
SICKBED

~❧~

July 17, 1903

THE DAY WAS warm and brilliant with light when Katrina entered the Daugherty house on Main Street with a bouquet of asters and zinnias just cut from her garden on Colonie Street: reds, oranges, pinks, and yellows to brighten the sickroom where Emmett Daugherty, eighty-one, lay dying of decay and disuse.

Katrina had come to see this as a house of death, for just before she and Edward stayed here, in the months the Colonie Street house was being renovated, Hanorah died of a heart seizure. And they were still here when Adelaide, Jacob, Cora, and all the others died from the fire. Now death was claiming yet another soul, and the imminence was giving meaning to Katrina's life in the way her vigil at Cora's exhumation had vitalized her days. The sun was shining brightly on this latest visitation.

The front door was open (Emmett had not locked it since he built the house) and Katrina strode into the hallway and past the front parlor, which had gone all but unused since Hanorah died. The parlor always seemed to Katrina to be Hanorah's museum: the rocking chair where she sat to sew, and to monitor the passersby on Main Street; the huge woodstove she always tended that was now ornamental with the advent of the coal furnace; the dusty valances, the chair doilies—when were they last washed?

She walked down the hallway into the kitchen, found two empty milk bottles in the pantry, and filled them with water and flowers. A woman in a housedress and a clean white apron that covered the dress from waist to ankle came in through the kitchen door. Who is she? A face Katrina knew. Annie Farrell, from next door, that's right. I haven't seen her since '95. So pretty. So plain. And not Farrell anymore.

"Mrs. Daugherty, I'm not interrupting, am I?" Annie said.

"Oh, hello, hello, not at all," said Katrina. I can't call her Annie. Mrs. Phelan? No. "I brought some flowers."

"So beautiful," Annie said. "And I baked some beans and bread, just out of the stove. I know nobody cooks in this house."

"That's sweet of you," said Katrina. She thinks I should come every day and cook?

"With all the sickness and trouble, I mean," Annie said. "How is he?"

"I just this minute got here. But I know he had a very bad night. Go up and say hello."

"I wouldn't intrude," Annie said.

"He'd love it. He speaks so fondly of the Farrells next door."

"There's always been a closeness. He and my father helped each other build their houses."

"But you're not a Farrell anymore," said Katrina.

"Right you are, Mrs. Daugherty. I'm a Phelan these four years. Francis, you know. He worships your husband."

"Yes." And I worshiped him. *Worshiped* Francis. Before you did, Mrs. Phelan.

"He always mentions your kindness when you were neighbors and he worked for you," Annie said.

"Does he? That's nice." Kindness he thinks it was?

Katrina picked up the two bottles with the flowers.

"We'll go see Emmett," she said, and Annie followed her up the stairs to the sickroom, where Edward, in his late-afternoon ritual, was sitting with Frank McArdle, the Daugherty family doctor, an ample-bellied man with a white brush of a mustache, here on his daily visit. Edward and the doctor were delivering up stories and gossip to keep Emmett alive with words alone. As the women entered they saw Emmett, raising phlegm from his ruined lungs, propped on pillows under a large colored likeness of Pope Leo XIII, the man Emmett loved better than Jesus.

Katrina remembered an angry Emmett invoking Leo when the trolley strike of 1901 was looming. He would rant over supper about the injustice of the traction company for bringing in scab labor and not only refusing its workers a pittance of a wage increase, but cutting their wages and extending their workday. She could see him pounding the table, bouncing potatoes out of the dish, declaiming to all: "Don't take my word. The Pope of Rome himself said it. Workers are not chattels, and it's shameful to treat them like that. Shameful, that's the Pope's word for those traction company frauds. 'To defraud anyone of wages that are his due is a crime that cries out to the avenging anger of heaven.' There's Pope Leo for you, a real man he is, and by the Jesus, no man ever spoke truer. Amen to Leo, I say. Amen to Leo."

Now Emmett lay beneath the image of the Workingman's Pope, his eyes half closed, giving fading attention to Dr. McArdle, who was talking of a woman who married a man for his money and the man then went bankrupt and stayed that way twelve years.

"It's a rare day," said the doctor, "that people marry for love anymore, the way you and I did, Emmett, and the way Edward did. Am I right, Edward?"

"I hear you, Frank," Edward said. "But love isn't enough, and anybody who thinks it is, is demented."

Katrina, hearing this as she entered, said, "You are so right, my love," and she put one bottle of flowers on Emmett's dresser, the other on his bedside table.

Edward took her aside, held her hand.

"There are impediments to love," she said softly.

"How well I know that," he said.

"I'm glad you accept it."

"I don't accept it."

"But you must," she said.

Edward pushed love away, whispered to her that Emmett was

very weak, and that they had decided to go for the priest. Emmett heard him.

"Yes, get Father Loonan," Emmett said with more strength than Katrina expected. "And have a pitcher of ale to pour when he gets here."

Annie Farrell walked to Emmett's bedside, touched his hand with her fingertips, shook her head.

"Giving drink to the priest, now is that a good thing, Emmett?"

Emmett almost smiled and answered her in such a scratchy whisper that Annie had to lean over to hear him.

"He says ale is God's greatest handiwork," Annie said.

"Then we should get some right away," said Edward.

"I'll get Father Loonan," Katrina said, "and then I'll stop for the ale."

"You?" said Annie. "You surely wouldn't be seen in a saloon."

"It's time I would be," Katrina said, and she bent over Emmett and kissed his forehead. "Don't you dare go anywhere till I get back," she said.

"I'll get the ale," Edward told her, "you get the priest."

"I'll get both," said Katrina. "You stay here with your father, where you ought to be."

In the kitchen Katrina rinsed out Emmett's two-quart pewter growler with the snap-on cover and put it in a wicker handbasket. Edward was right about love. The impulse to love is a disease. Is disease a proper reason for marrying? No sane person would do anything for such love. What had loving Francis meant? When he went away she was left with dead memories, cold as a corpse. Try drawing love out of a corpse. It's never who or what you love that drives you, Katrina, but who or what loves you. A cat. If a cat loves me, I am alive.

She left the house and walked the two and a half blocks to Sacred Heart church on Walter Street, the church Emmett helped build with his monthly payments and the strength of his back. She rang the parish house bell to rouse Father Loonan, who had performed the marriage ceremony for Edward and Katrina seventeen years ago. He opened the door, fresh from his prayers, or was it a nap? Well, he seemed to be elsewhere.

"Emmett Daugherty is dying, Father. He needs you. He needs the sacrament."

"Ah, the poor devil, he's all done, is he?"

"He's no devil, Father. He's a virtuous man."

"Oh he is, he is. I've got someone coming in ten minutes, my dear, and then I'll be along."

"Emmett can't wait ten minutes, Father."

"He can't. It's that way, is it?"

"Your visitor can wait, but Emmett is losing the light."

"Then I'll be right along, dear, right along."

"Excellent, Father," Katrina said, and turned to leave.

"Have you candlesticks in the house?" the priest asked.

"I believe we do."

"And a crucifix. You must have a crucifix."

"We have one."

"Holy water. Do you have that?"

"We do."

"And the chrism?"

"The what, Father?"

"The chrism, child. The holy oil."

"I never saw any."

"Then I'll bring it. And a piece of palm from Palm Sunday. You must have that."

"There's some stuck behind Jesus on the crucifix."

"All right. And a lemon, do you have a lemon?"

"I'll buy one if we don't."

"And water, and a spoon, I'll need that."

"Are you going to make lemonade, Father?"

"Don't get flibbertigibbet on me," the priest said. "And a piece of cotton. And some bread. And salt."

"We'll have it all," Katrina said.

"Then we'll get Emmett ready for his journey," Father Loonan said.

Katrina left him in the doorway and walked toward Jack McCall's saloon on Broadway. Lemon and cotton and salt and oil. What a peculiar religion she had joined, its mysteries endless. She walked with a dynamic erectness, straight back, narrow waist, wide-brimmed straw hat flat on her yellow hair, her walk, almost a military pace, surging with the energy of youth, though she was now thirty-seven. She moved toward McCall's with an all-but-visible purpose, a change of mood for Katrina, who did daily battle with absence of purpose, boredom, pervasive ambivalence toward every waking act. Why should I get up? Why go to bed? Why try to reimagine Francis? Why write the diary? Why not? It's as meaningful as anything else you might do, and as meaningless. You have a lazy soul, Katrina. You will die with such slowness, such slight daily reduction, that no one will notice that you've left the room until the clusters of dust accumulate around your empty chair.

But today could be different: today on Main Street, at the parish house, heading for the saloon, immersed in the life of the people you inherited when you wed Edward, today you know that change is so real it can almost be touched. You will be free, Katrina, when you know what drives you. When Emmett, that wonderful man, at last ceases to linger, you will be liberated from the street that marriage has imposed upon you. Won't you be free? I do love my husband and his family. I do, I do. And I do think them alien to all that I am or will be.

There were no saloons like McCall's in Katrina's private domain. She entered it through the front door, walked to the bar and put the basket on top of it. As she lifted out the growler, the bartender and six men at the bar stared at her. This was a small, two-room saloon with black window curtains that were closed only on Sunday mornings, when it was illegal to serve spirits to any but the neediest cases. Such cases entered as quickly as possible through the side door, for you wouldn't be seen going into a saloon's front door on a Sunday. Also, women always entered through that same side door, the ladies' entrance, and sat at one of three tables in the back room, where ladies were supposed to sit. And not for long.

"We don't have women at the bar, Ma'am," the bartender said. His name was Jimmy McGrath and he had managed the saloon for Jack McCall ever since Jack became a county undersheriff. Jimmy was known as the most honest bartender in Albany, for no drunk ever lost the money he didn't know he'd left on Jimmy's bar. Jimmy would put it in the register, with a note specifying the credit, and he'd tell the drunk about it on his next visit. Katrina did not know such things about Jimmy, but she liked his kindly face, and the clever way he parted the remains of his silky white hair.

"I don't plan to stay," she said to Jimmy. "I only want this filled with ale," and she pushed the growler toward him. He didn't touch it.

"Ladies generally come in the other door and sit in the ladies' section," he said. "And ladies never come in without an escort. For politeness and protection."

"I shall be very polite, I assure you. And I need no protection."

"Ladies sit back there, Ma'am, no matter what."

"Is there a bar back there where I can get my ale?"

"No, Ma'am. This is the only bar."

"Then I'll stay here, and when I get it I'll leave."

"But we don't serve ladies here, Ma'am. House rule."

"And a silly one, I must say. My father-in-law is dying, and the ale is for him, and for Father Loonan when he comes to perform the last rites, ten minutes from now."

The men nodded at the solemnity of use to which this ale was about to be put.

"You probably know the man who's dying," Katrina said. "Emmett Daugherty is his name."

"Ah, Emmett. So that's who it is," Jimmy said. "I knew he was ailing."

"Emmett is dying?" said one of the men. He was tall and brawny and wore a brown derby with a hole in it. He took off his hat, looked at it reverentially, then put it back on. "I've known him all my life. A grand man."

"He's very close to death," Katrina said. "Now may I have this container filled?" She put a dollar on the bar.

Jimmy McGrath uncovered the growler, put it under the ale spigot, and pushed the dollar back to Katrina.

"Tell Emmett this round is on Jimmy," he said.

He capped the full growler, put it in Katrina's basket, lifted it and came around the bar to hand it to her.

Outside, a dog yelped in pain. Katrina looked out to see a man kicking a collie dog tied to the tailgate of a wagon loaded with red bricks.

"That man is kicking a dog," Katrina said, and all the men came to the window to look at the spectacle. The man kicked the dog again. A heavyset woman, sitting on the wagon and holding the reins of the two horses, watched the kicking.

"Somebody should stop him," Katrina said. "Help that poor animal that can't help itself."

"Yes, Ma'am," said the tall man with the derby. He went out the saloon's screen door and spoke to the dog-kicker.

"You oughtn'ta kick that dog," said the tall man.

"It's my dog. I'll kick him all I want," said the dog-kicker, and he kicked the dog again. He was short and muscular from lifting bricks, and he wore a sleeveless undershirt.

The tall man effortlessly shoved him to one side, then reached down and untied the rope that held the dog. The dog ran away. Katrina came out of the saloon with her basket.

"You did very well," she said to the tall man. "I thank you, and I'm sure the dog does too."

"You better go bring my dog back," the dog-kicker said.

"No, I ain't gonna do that," the tall man said. "You'd only kick him some more."

The dog-kicker swung his fist, but the blow only reached the left side of the tall man's neck. The tall man threw two short, powerful punches, one with each hand, and knocked the dog-kicker backward into the street. When he went down, the back of his head hit the granite-block pavement. He started to sit up but fell back and stayed down. Everybody stared at him. The woman climbed off the wagon. She was as burly as the man on the ground (Katrina thought of them as a matched pair), and wore a man's shirt with sleeves rolled, her muscular arms bare well above the elbow. She lifted the fallen man up onto the sidewalk and raised him with a hand under his back. His head wobbled.

"You killed him," the woman yelled at the tall man.

"I didn't kill him," the tall man said. "He hit me and I hit him."

"He shouldn't have kicked the dog," Katrina said.

"Who asked you?" the woman said. "Maybe he shoulda kicked you. Maybe I oughta kick your tail across Broadway."

"I'm harder to kick than a tied-up dog," Katrina said.

"You think so?" the woman said, and she flexed her right bicep, the size of a grapefruit, and walked toward Katrina. She tightened the muscle and held it and the veins stood out like branches of a tree. She stared at Katrina and tensed the muscle, splitting a vein and spurting blood onto Katrina's yellow dress; then she raised the bloody bicep in front of Katrina's face.

"I don't have to kick you," the woman said. "I'll squeeze you like a bunch of grapes."

The tall man stepped between the women. "Nobody gonna squeeze this lady."

"I'm gettin' the cops after you, Mister," the woman said.

"That's good," said the tall man. "I'll be waitin' for 'em here in the saloon. You go along, now, Miss," he told Katrina. "This ain't your business to worry about."

"If you need a witness, my name is Katrina Daugherty. Second-last house on Main Street."

"Okay, Miss Daugherty, and we thank you," the tall man said. He tipped his hat. "You tell Emmett, but only if he's really dyin', that Hoggie Ryan wishes him a happy death."

"Does he know you, Mr. Ryan?"

"He seen me fight bare-knuckle many a night."

"I shall certainly tell him. Hoggie Ryan. Thank you."

Katrina shook hands with Hoggie and then walked toward Ronan's grocery to buy a lemon. She saw the collie sitting in the shade of a porch. As she passed, the dog wagged its tail.

Katrina put a chiffon scarf around her shoulders to hide the blood on her blouse; then she and Annie carried the ale and three glasses to Emmett's room. Katrina gave a glass to Edward, one to Dr. McArdle, and put one on a table for Father Loonan, drawing an instant rebuke from Emmett.

"Do you think I wouldn't have a glass meself?" he asked. "And one for each of you." The speech cost him strength, and he coughed, and slumped, then closed his eyes to rest for the next challenge.

"I'll go," Annie said, and while she went for more glasses, Katrina spread a white table scarf on Emmett's bedside table, then set out the paraphernalia Father Loonan requested: the holy water, a tablespoon, glass of water, wad of cotton, salt cellar, heel of bread, lemon sliced in two, two candleholders with blessed candles, the crucifix, and the palm fronds she undid from behind the torso of

Jesus. The table was so crowded that she and Edward brought down a long table from the attic to give proper space to the final necessities.

When Annie came in with the glasses Emmett opened his eyes. "Is no one goin' to pour the ale?" he asked.

"At your service," said Dr. McArdle, and he poured for those in the room, giving the first to Emmett, who took the glass and looked at it, then set it beside a blessed candle.

"I think you did this just to have a drink your doctor couldn't object to," Katrina said. "You don't look like you're dying."

"Half me life I didn't look like I was livin'. It evens out," Emmett said. And he closed his eyes again.

When Annie came back with Father Loonan, Doc McArdle poured an ale and handed it to him.

"What's this?" the priest asked.

"I know you like your ale," Emmett said.

"I never denied it," the priest said. "But I never had any with the last rites."

"It goes good with everything," Emmett said.

"Emmett Martin Daugherty," Edward said, "we're all present and accounted for. What's your pleasure? Where would you like your body anointed first, on the inside or the outside?"

"First I want to know what he does with that lemon," Emmett said.

"It cleans the oil off my fingers," the priest said.

"That's clever," Emmett said. He reached for the ale and raised the glass to the light. "By God that looks good. We'll just have a taste." He took a sip and others in the room did likewise. "All right," Emmett said, "get it over with."

"I was told you were dying," the priest said. "But I'm not sure you're dying."

"That's what I told him, Father," Katrina said.

"I'm dyin' nevertheless," Emmett said. "I can't stand on me pins anymore, and with every breath there's a pain, and when I close me eyes I see somethin' comin'."

"What does it look like?" the priest asked.

"Like the inside of a fireman's boot."

"That's not what heaven looks like."

"Then I'm goin' someplace else."

"Since you're able to talk, we'll want to have a confession," the priest said, and turning to the others he said, "If you'd all please leave the room . . ."

"There's no need," Emmett said. "I've nothin' to confess."

"You're a saint, then, is that it?" the priest said.

"Not hardly, but I've nothin' to confess."

"Confess the sins you forgot and I'll forgive those."

"I forgot none I ever committed. The memory of them kept me smiling for forty-five years."

"I'll forgive those. Anything else?"

"I let my wife work too hard."

"You've got company on that one."

"And I thought too little of meself," Emmett said. "I paid too much attention to the work, and the trees in the yard, and Reilly the dog, God rest his soul."

"Dogs don't have souls," the priest said.

"This one did," said Emmett. "He went to mass every Sunday with me. And he never ate meat on Friday."

"And did he do his Easter duty?"

"He did. On the parish house lawn."

"Is that all the sins?"

"I could make some up," Emmett said.

"No need for that," and he made the sign of the cross, saying, "*Te absolvo in nomine Patris et Filii et Spiritus Sancti.* For your penance say one Hail Mary and have some more ale."

Emmett blessed himself, closed his eyes for a ten-second prayer, then reached for his glass and took one long swallow, all he could tolerate. Father Loonan did likewise, then opened his prayer book and said, "Now we'll get on with it," and, holding the holy oil, read in the Latin: *"Per istam sanctam Unctionem, et suam piissimam misericordiam, indulgeat tibi Dominus quidquid deliquisti . . ."*

Emmett said to him, "Will ye say it in English so I know what's goin' on."

And the priest spoke the formal prayers of Extreme Unction, anointing, with holy oil on cotton, Emmett's eyes, ears, nose, lips, hands, and feet, the sensory entrances of sin, saying to him, "Through this holy Unction, and of His tender mercy, may the Lord pardon thee whatsoever sins thou hast committed by thine eyes . . . thine ears," and repeating it on through to the chrismal swabbing of the foot from heel to toe, whereupon Emmett spoke up and said, "There's no need to bother with the toes. I never sinned with any of them."

Katrina giggled, then broke into sobs she tried to stifle. This gallant man really was dying and by loving him she felt like a traitor to her own dead, for he loathed her father and spiritually worked against him all his life, and against the world that had shaped her family and her life. She looked at Edward and her sobbing intensified: my husband who put my sister and father in their graves, guiltless, honorable man now losing his own father. And all her love for Edward seemed remarkable and perverse. This Main Street, this North End, where the Daugherty seed took root, was, in all its guises, a foreign place, and yet its river and its foundries and its traction barns and its Lumber District and its dying canal were the sources of life that sustained *her* family in all its lineages—the Staatses, Bradfords, Taylors, Fitzgibbons, Van Slykes. Here were the wellsprings of power and wealth that had gilded the heart, soul, and lifetime of Katrina Taylor Daugherty, weeping child of the new century, wounded by the flames of hellish flowers, who can now find no substitute in life for her loss, her diminishment, her abasement known so intimately: loving and losing Francis Phelan, that angry, lovely boy who defeated the abstraction of power with a flung stone. Katrina, faithless, sobbing wretch, you are adrift in this Irish Catholic fog that envelops your elegantly patrician self. (That woman with the bloody bicep must be Catholic. She would be all wrong as an Episcopalian.) What does your poet say to you now, Katrina? He says that the world goes round by misunderstanding, the only way people can agree: for if they understood each other they would never agree on anything, such as marriage to the enemy: that man across the room whom you say you love, who woke you into a terrifying nightmare, who had you screaming for release before you even made the bond with him, who led you, docile woman, out of fire into salvation; that man who is the son of this virtuous man dying in front of you. What part of this dying father has passed into that living son, do you know? When the soul's light goes out forever, what is the loss to those who have stood for so long in that light? Your sobs are evidence of an uncertain mind, Katrina. You should not cry at the death of a beloved man to whom you once gave only hostility. Your allegiance is as fickle as the rain. Your giggle at his sinless toes is a proper response.

The priest ended the sacrament and made the sign of the cross over Emmett. Katrina breathed in, straightened her back, and raised her glass in emulation of Edward's celebratory gesture.

"All praise to Emmett Daugherty," she said. "All praise to a great man, I say. The truly great men are the poet, the priest, and the soldier, and Emmett Daugherty is a soldier of the righteous wars."

Then, between sobs, she willfully drank all of her ale.

"CULLY WATSON HANGED"

Albany Argus, *May 24, 1910*

CULBERT (CULLY) WATSON, known in Albany for years as a hotel sneak and petty hoodlum, was hanged from a telegraph pole in the French Quarter of New Orleans last night after being taken off a train at gunpoint by four men in kerchief masks. Watson was en route to New Orleans for trial on an attempted-murder charge, and was in custody of two New Orleans detectives when the four masked men disarmed and tied up the detectives, and fled the train with Watson.

His corpse was found hanging on Bourbon Street, near the hotel where ten days ago, police say, he raped, robbed, and left for dead a twenty-seven-year-old woman. She had been smothered, but revived to find the room filled with gas from an open jet. She said she'd seen her attacker working at the hotel desk as night clerk. Police said the attacker had gained entry to and left the woman's room through the transom, and that Watson was slim and agile enough to accomplish this. He has a known history of such unlawful entry and assault on women.

Police caught Watson with the woman's diamond brooch and $2,000 in cash as he stepped off a train at Memphis. To bargain with police, Watson told of his connection to the infamous Love Nest killings of 1908, when a prominent Albany physician, Giles Fitzroy, murdered his wife, shot and wounded the Albany playwright Edward Daugherty, then killed himself. The shootings took place at the Millerton House in Manhattan, where Watson was then working. He disappeared after the killings.

Police said Dr. Fitzroy and Daugherty testified against Watson at a hearing into a river-barge brawl in 1906, and Watson may have held a grudge against them. Police have a lengthy statement from Watson about the Love Nest case but have disclosed no details about Watson's role in it; but they did say that others may be involved.

A PICNIC ON THE BARGE

June 17, 1906

EDWARD, IN HIS white suit and white Panama with the flowerpot crown, walked at sunbright morning with a stream of other men, women, and children down Columbia Street past the new Union Station. Where the goddamned Delavan stood. Handsome new building and they used plenty of the Delavan's scorched bricks. Some things can be salvaged from any wreckage. Katrina?

He headed toward the old red bridge that spanned the Albany Basin, then out toward the pier, where two covered, double-deck barges, and the tug that would pull them, rested at anchor in the placid water of the Hudson. He saw Maginn coming toward the bridge from another direction, and he waited for him.

"You're alone," Maginn said.

"So are you," said Edward.

"I'm always alone, except when I'm with a beautiful and accessible woman, which I fully expect to be before this day is over."

"My own beautiful woman decided not to come."

"That's truly a pity," Maginn said. "How is she? I haven't seen her in months."

"She's all right. You know she doesn't favor the drinking."

Despite Edward's arguments to Katrina that today they could celebrate something *together* for a change—the river's summer glory, the gift of a lustrous day—she said she couldn't abide all that family sweetness, all those dowdy biddies, all the rowdiness. So she stayed home. Avoiding the class struggle.

"Then we're a couple of bachelors for the day," Maginn said. "Like the old days. Tent city at the State Fair, when you were still a lowly reporter? Remember?"

"Things have changed since then," Edward said.

"Not I. I find myself a lowly reporter still. And I still dandle the doxies, don't you, old man, once in a while, just for the hell of it? Tell the truth."

"Part of my past," Edward said.

"You've tamed the tendril. How resolute."

At the gangway, a policeman was backing a man down the ramp, poking his chest with a billy club. Five others backed down behind him. Edward recognized the cop, Willie Glass.

"It's not a free ride," Glass said. "Buy a ticket."

"Go scratch your ass, Glass," said the ejected man, who was short, wiry, and thirtyish, with long black hair parted in the middle, a full mustache, and sufficiently irregular good looks that Edward judged him a pimp. He mumbled to the men with him and they went away.

"Sheridan Avenue boys," Maginn said. "The one sassing the cop is Cully Watson. He doesn't like to pay for things."

"He has the look of a man who uses women," Edward said.

"Very perceptive," Maginn said. "He's also very wild."

Edward and Maginn boarded the barge for the impending voyage, a neighborhood outing of North and South End church groups, social clubs, and singing societies. They'd all been accumulating food in their club rooms and vestries for days for this, the Eintracht excursion, which took its name from the city's premier choral group, the Eintracht Singing Society, a mix of working and professional men, Protestants and Catholics, Germans, Dutch, English, and Irish, who once a year embarked together on this exercise in social leveling.

The excursion was financed by boarding tickets, and the sale of prepaid tickets for beer and soft drinks. People had been boarding since eight o'clock, fifty cents a head; and the two barges (used to haul ice, hay, or produce on weekdays) were already a floating small town. At ten-thirty, with more than two thousand aboard, the sailors hauled up the gangway. *Old Hellhound*, the tug, towed the first barge under and past the narrow draws of the Maiden Lane and South Ferry Street bridges, then went back for the second barge; and when the two were side by side, sailors lashed them together, then opened the rails of their top decks so the two boats became one, doubling the conviviality. Then the tug moved them downriver at low speed, toward the Baerena Island picnic grounds.

Edward and Maginn searched for a table on a lower deck, where women were already passing out knockwurst, pork sandwiches, plates of beans and cabbage, and men were clustered at the bar, where two bartenders steadily drew mugs of beer from tapped kegs. Johnny Daugherty, the famous fiddler, Edward's distant cousin through unchartable family links in Spiddal, broke into "The Wind That Shakes the Barley" for anyone ready to jig this early in the day, and there were a few. Card games proceeded, and Edward saw Midge Kresser unfolding his portable three-card-monte table, about to begin his day's work parting suckers from their nickels and dimes. Ministers and priests were eating with their flocks. Policemen Willie Glass and Joe Anthony strolled the deck, keeping the peace.

"I see Giles," Edward said, and they found him in line for drinks, wearing his commodore's cap and lemon-yellow vest.

"Felicity come with you?" Edward asked, expecting Giles's wife would have absented herself today for the same reasons as Katrina.

"She did," Giles said, and he pointed toward a table where Felicity was sitting with a woman in her late forties. Felicity was quintessentially summery in a white linen frock and white straw boater with pink ribbon. The other woman was older, slender, bosomy, and narrow-waisted, her pale-green dress subtly décolleté.

"That woman with your wife," Maginn said, "she's suitable for a saddle, wouldn't you say, Fitz?"

"I knew you'd notice her, Maginn," Giles said. "Felicity's Aunt

Sally, a handsome woman. To tell the truth, I wouldn't be surprised if she went for you. She has a weakness for your type."

"What's my type?"

"Worthless lout with a wit," Giles said. "Her husband has no sense of humor."

"She has a husband but fancies witty men."

"I hear he's not much of a husband. He's a fire chief down in Westchester. You see before you the fireman's wife."

"The fireman's wife. And why is she here?"

"Visiting Felicity. The fire chief rents a summer place near Glenmont, and Sally stays there all summer. The chief comes up weekends."

"Weekends," said Maginn. "Is that a midweek knock at the door I hear?"

"I wouldn't go so fast," Giles said. "She's a proper lady all the same."

"Of course. Aren't they all?"

Giles's procuring for his wife's aunt at first mention of her existence baffled Edward. It was out of character for the man, but it certainly energized Maginn.

"What do you want to do, Maginn? As if I didn't know."

"I'll go chat with Giles," Maginn said.

"You do that," Edward said. "I'll see you later."

And Edward then roamed the barge alone, seeing who was aboard. He saw Jack McCall sitting with Ruthie, and Father Loonan with a glass of ale in front of him, and men Edward knew from the Eintracht, to which he, Giles, and Maginn all belonged. Lyman had initiated Edward into the singing group at age sixteen ("The Daughertys always had the music" was Emmett's line), but as he grew older, traveling as a writer, Edward lost connection with the group, except for this excursion. He had no desire now to join anybody's company. The fraternal impulse to spend the day with his fellow Eintrachters and North Enders, to celebrate family serenity and midsummer's sweet pleasures, had faded totally. If he could get off the barge now, he would.

He heard half a dozen singers in an impromptu rendering of "Believe Me, If All Those Endearing Young Charms," Tom Moore's ballad about the constancy of love:

Thou wouldst still be adored,
As this moment thou art,
Let thy loveliness fade as it will . . .

He walked to the rail and felt the day warming, saw the sky as a wash of peaceable blue. He stared out at a field full of grazing cows, at the great trees along the river's edge, at the riverfront mansions, and fields of early-sprouting corn growing above the floodplain, and he felt invincibly depressed, trapped in his shriveling skin: a man in motion to save himself from stasis. Tom Moore's song mocked what he felt about his increasingly silent marriage. The only constancy was Katrina's steady withdrawal into her world of poetry and fantasy, the endless interiorizing of her life in diaries, which she did not hide, but which Edward would not intrude upon. Her behavior had been eccentric always, but after the Delavan she backpedaled into silence, her life a chamber of secrets and venerations of all that is sad and solitary: in communion is contamination; in isolation the suffering soul's beauty is enhanced.

"Where have you gone?" he had asked her this morning after she decided not to join him on the excursion.

"Where I have to be," she said.

"You should be here with me."

"I am here."

"You're not."

"Let me be."

"I apologize for trying to make you look at us as we are, and what we have become. I know it's terrible to force someone to accept reality."

She smiled and grew more beautiful.

Francis Phelan tapped him on the shoulder.

"You ain't thinkin' of jumpin' overboard, are you, Ed?"

Edward shook hands with Francis.

"Just thinking about things that can spoil a great day," Edward said. "How come you're not playing ball?"

"We got us a day off and Annie wanted to spend it on the river."

Francis, maybe the best baseball player in the city, played shortstop for Albany in the New York State League. Edward had written a play, *The Car Barns,* about the Albany trolley strike of 1901, and modeled his hero on Francis, a young man who, with uncanny accuracy, threw a stone the size of a baseball and killed a scab motorman, an action that started the riot in which the militia killed two men, unacceptable violence in defense of scabs that hastened a strike settlement and made Francis a hero of the strikers.

"Your family all okay?" Francis asked. "Katrina and Martin?"

"They're fine," said Edward, looking at Francis now as Katrina seemed to see him: her bauble when he'd lived next door to the Daughertys on Colonie Street, before he married Annie Farrell: handsome young handyman in whose presence Katrina went fluttery. Very thrilling, no doubt. You know, said La Voluptueuse, I'm only interested in youth.

"Martin's started to write stories, father's footsteps," Edward said.

"He can do it. Smart kid like Martin puts his mind to it, he could stand on his ear, do anything he wants."

"Sometimes it's not that easy."

"Maybe not," Francis said. "Can I buy you a beer? I got too many tickets in my pocket."

"No thanks, Fran."

"That play you wrote," Francis said. "People always tell me it's me and your father."

"It's some of you and him, all right, but not really."

In the play the hero is counseled by a labor organizer, as Emmett had counseled the young Francis, told him about the Pittsburgh steel mills, and the Sons of Vulcan Emmett had helped organize to give voice to the workers. "Identify the enemy," the organizer keeps saying in the play, and the hero identifies one with a stone.

"I ain't no godalmighty hero for what I did and never thought I was," Francis said. "I had a good time watchin' your play, but I sure don't talk like that hero."

"You have your own eloquence, Francis, and people know it. You're a fellow to reckon with."

"I learned a lot from Emmett. Most clearheaded man I ever come across. Anything I asked him he had an answer. You don't find people like that. They're a gift. One day you get lucky and meet one, and after a while you find out you're halfway smart, smarter'n you ever thought you'd be."

"Emmett was serious about every day of his life."

"That's the truth. I'm serious too. If the Daughertys ever need anything, I'm there."

Edward nodded and thought: I'll pass the word to Katrina.

When he went back to Giles's table, the women were gone, Maginn and Giles were sitting with Jimmy Cadden, another Eintrachter, a prankster who battened on the comic discomfiture of his friends, especially Maginn.

"Where's Aunt Sally and Felicity?" Edward asked.

"Maginn chased them away," Cadden said.

"Not true," said Maginn. "I paid them such compliments they couldn't sit still. Sally is crazy about me."

"She thinks Maginn is demented," Cadden said.

"We'll see what she thinks," Maginn said.

"Let's say Sally was amused," said Giles.

"I saw you talking to the hero of your play," Maginn said to Edward.

"If you mean Francis Phelan, get it right," Edward said. "He inspired part of the hero's character, but only part."

"The radical part," Maginn said.

"Some of that, yes," Edward said.

"How's that play doing?" Giles asked.

"Played to sold-out houses in Albany for a month and a half last year," Edward said. "Did well in Boston and Philadelphia, and it's still running in New York."

"I'm writing about it for the *Century*," Maginn said, "an article on using fiction and theater for political ends, writers telling us how the world ought to be. I seriously warn you against running with those pimps of transformation, Edward. You're a talented man, and *The Car Barns* is a talented play, but radical work like that strikes me as a justification for labor violence. I'm fond of politics, but let's not call it art."

"Some art is political, whether you like it or not."

"And some plays are so political they cease to be art."

"I write what I believe. My soul is open for inspection."

"Read my inspection report on your soul in the *Century*."

"What about *your* novel? When do we get a look at it?"

"Let's say my novel is in abeyance," Maginn said.

"You've quit it," said Edward.

"Maybe," said Maginn.

Excellent move, Edward thought. You never wrote a fictional paragraph I believed. More intelligent than talented, that's your condition, Maginn.

"We all do some things better than others," Edward said.

"I envy you your naïveté, Edward," Maginn said. "You still think that everything you do matters. I think it's all a chase after the great cipher."

"Time to chase the beer," Cadden said.

"I'll go," Maginn said, and he collected the drinkers' prepaid beer tickets. When he moved toward the bar, Giles quickly unfurled his plan for the Fireman's Wife Joke. He'd heard about it in New York, where it had had great success, but now said he needed Cadden and Edward to make it work.

"Leave me out," Edward said. "I'm too old for this."

"Of course you are. That's what makes you credible."

Edward was only five years older than Giles, but five seemed like twenty to Edward. Giles, dedicated physician, good and amiable friend, was the perennial adolescent, a fireman himself since the Delavan, reveling in the excitement of a flaming building, riding with firefighters as their doctor, treating injured firemen and burn victims.

"What do you expect me to do?" Edward asked him.

"Be the voice of authority."

"Who else are you bringing in on it?"

"Somebody whose voice Maginn won't recognize. Clubber Dooley, maybe. Maginn doesn't know Clubber very well."

"Can you trust Clubber not to give it away?" Cadden asked. "Isn't his brain a little wrinkled?"

"Clubber'll do me a favor," Giles said. "I eased the pain in his bad foot last year."

"Maginn is smart," Edward said. "He'll figure it out."

"Maybe not," Cadden said. "When he's hot for a woman his brain moves below his belt."

Very accurate on Maginn, Edward thought. The man, unfortunately, was a freak. He could be the greatest of friends, great talker, witty and oddly wise. Edward had had misgivings asking him to be best man at the wedding, but Maginn behaved impeccably, a notable contributor to the elevated spirits of that marvelous day. And he was embarrassingly grateful for being asked: an imprimatur on the friendship. But you are also a pain in the ass, Maginn. Your mouth is out of control and so is your critical faculty. You need comeuppance. Edward decided to help with the joke.

Maginn returned with the news that a roll of the prepaid tickets used for buying beer had been stolen, and bartenders were accepting only cash. Maginn, short of cash, suggested they all buy their own drinks. So he, Cadden, and Edward moved toward the bar at the stern of the barge.

Cully Watson and the five other toughs from the gangway incident, all in their twenties, all in shirtsleeves and caps, hovered near the bar. Only Watson was bareheaded. He had an empty glass in one hand and tickets in the other.

"You're saying my money's no good," Watson said.

"Tickets are no good," the bartender said. "Our tickets were stolen. You want a beer, you pay cash."

"I paid cash for these tickets when I got on this shitbucket."

"Maybe you did, but now it's cash only."

"He says our tickets are no good," Watson said to his friends.

"Maybe he's the one that's no good," said one.

"He says he only takes cash," Watson said.

Edward saw the toughs were already in a fight stance, coiled with energy. Watson's talk was a gambit. Cadden stepped up to the bar.

"I got cash money and I'd like three lagers," Cadden said. He turned to Watson. "You guys don't mind, do you?"

The barman filled three mugs. Watson stared at Cadden.

"This is trouble," Maginn said. "Let it go, Cadden. We'll go to the bar on the upper deck."

"I got 'em already," Cadden said, reaching for the beers.

"You wait your turn," Watson said, and he put his tickets on the bar. "I'll take them beers."

"Not with tickets you won't," the bartender said, and he pushed the beers closer to Cadden. Watson reached for the mugs but Cadden blocked him.

"You ain't very polite," Watson said. He shoved Cadden with one hand and knocked him off-balance, then swept the mugs off the bar.

"Bad news, Cadden, I told you," Maginn said. "Don't push it."

"Cheap hooligan," Cadden said.

As Cadden faced down Watson, one tough picked up a fallen beer mug and stood staring at him. Suddenly the tough swung the mug and hit Cadden on the side of the head. He staggered and fell across the bar. Willie Glass and Joe Anthony arrived, swinging nightsticks. Glass rapped the tough who had floored Cadden and he buckled. Maginn and Edward pulled Cadden away from the bar and sat him on a bench. Edward felt his head. No blood. Cadden shook his head, trying to focus.

"Break this up," Willie Glass was saying, shoving the toughs away from the bar. He and Joe Anthony had their backs to each other as they swung their clubs.

"I'll get that son of a bitch," Cadden said.

"Cadden," Maginn whispered, "that's Cully Watson. He's a killer."

"Where's Giles? Get Giles to come and look at Cadden's head," Edward said to Maginn.

Two toughs leaped on Glass, took away his stick, and brought him down. Two other toughs were showing knives, and one said, "The cop says break it up, so we'll break it up," and he kicked Glass in the mouth, then bashed his face with a beer mug. Anthony clubbed the kicker, but another tough hit Anthony with a mug and blood spurted from his left eye.

Two fell on Glass, punching his face, which was drenched in blood. One tough took his revolver and two others pulled off his uniform jacket, then his pants and shoes. Jack McCall moved out of the crowd and next to Edward, a club in his hand.

"Let's move in," Jack said.

"Gimme his gun," Cully Watson said, and a tough threw Glass's gun to Cully, who fired it into the deck, halting Jack and Edward's forward motion. Another tough took Anthony's pistol and pulled his uniform off. With their knives the toughs sliced the uniforms into rags. Cully, pistol in hand, shoved aside the two elderly bartenders, and with his other hand held a mug under the open tap.

One tough pointed Anthony's pistol at the crowd of picnickers, keeping reinforcements at bay. Men from the excursion sent women and children to the upper deck.

Cully drew more beers and slid them across the bar to the toughs, who guzzled it. Cully left the taps open, the deck awash in beer, then tucked the pistol in his belt, picked up an empty keg, and tossed it over the bar to a tough, who caught it.

"Give Glass some beer," Cully said, and the tough dropped the beer keg on Willie Glass's back. Glass was unconscious, clad only in underwear, his and Anthony's uniforms in shreds. Anthony was conscious, but bleeding profusely.

"Take a uniform away from a cop," Cully said, "you can't tell he's a cop no more."

Edward saw Francis moving up behind the tough who held the pistol, and he decided to act.

"You goddamn pack of jackals," Edward yelled, and he threw a beer mug at the tough with the gun and hit his chin. The man fired once and hit a stranger next to Edward. Francis came up behind the tough and pinioned him with a life preserver, then kneed him in the crotch and kicked the gun toward Edward. Cully fired a second shot into the deck before Edward could pick up the pistol. Another tough rushed to pick it up, but Cadden, with the energy of rage, stood and grabbed the attacker's arm, smashed his nose with his fist. Cadden snapped the man's arm like an ear of corn, dragged him to the railing.

"Let's move," Cully yelled, and he fired again into the deck. The toughs backed away from the bar as Cadden flung the man with the broken arm into the river.

Edward picked up the fallen gun as Black Jack and men from the crowd with knives and clubs moved toward Cully and crew. Cully led his toughs up a ladder, firing over the heads of the crowd as they went. Nobody followed them.

Giles was suddenly there as Edward and Maginn lifted the wounded stranger and the two savaged policemen onto tables where Giles could treat their wounds. Edward saw Maginn going up the ladder the toughs had climbed.

Word reached the captain and he pulled his tug close to a man in a rowboat to tell him of the riot on board and to send a message to the Albany police. The captain turned the tug and the barges in a semicircle and moved at high speed back toward Albany. Edward saw the rowboat man pulling the tough with the broken arm out of the water.

Edward thought: When you look at Cully Watson you know what you're looking at, but when you look at Maginn you don't know what he's become since yesterday. You could not know he would follow Cully and his gang, which scattered among the crowds on the four decks of the two barges. You might have predicted that by the time the Albany police rowed out to the barges at the Columbia Street pier, Cully and his toughs would be elsewhere. But you could not have predicted that Maginn would row Cully to the Rensselaer shore across from Albany, then row back to the barge.

When Maginn climbed back aboard from the lifeboat, he said he'd found Cully at the stern of the second barge, taking up slack on the rope of the lifeboat that trailed the barge in the water. Cully told Maginn to drop into the boat and row him and the boys ashore or he'd shoot him.

"What could I do?" Maginn asked.

"Why couldn't he row himself?" Edward asked.

"He wanted to see who was following him."

"Why didn't he have one of his pals row?"

"He thinks they're stupid."

"But you're intelligent enough to row a boat."

"Cully doesn't like me, and you don't argue with a man with a pistol."

"Why doesn't he like you?"

"Something I wrote about him in the paper."

"Will you write about this?"

"Of course."

"Naming names?"

"Do you think I'm suicidal?"

A police sergeant, finding no culprits on either barge, arrested Maginn for aiding a felon, and for taking a lifeboat from a river vessel, a federal offense. As police led Maginn away, Felicity's aunt waved a handkerchief at him, and Maginn, in hand chains, vigorously waved back with both hands.

Edward and Giles posted bail for Maginn, but after his interrogation, the charges against him were dropped. Cully left Albany a fugitive, the only one of the gang known by name. At a hearing Edward and Giles testified to the beating of the police, and to one tough's shooting a man in the crowd. Police arrested three men, but ten witnesses in their behalf testified they were sunning themselves on an upper deck during the fight. No other witness came forward to testify against the wild boys, and all charges were dismissed: a victory for numerical perjury, and triumph of the worst and the least.

Maginn never wrote about the brawl for *The Argus*. His editor said nobody believed his rowboat-kidnapping story.

COURTING THE FIREMAN'S WIFE

July 1, 1906

TWO WEEKS AFTER the excursion Giles called Edward to say Cadden's head was mended, and they were ready to play. They all met at Keeler's men's bar and Giles revealed that Sally would welcome a visit from Maginn tonight, after nine o'clock, when the house was empty. She wanted to hear of Maginn's encounter with the hoodlums, and had heard he was a writer, as was she. She was writing a love story on the order of *Wuthering Heights*.

"Where are these rooms she's taken?" Maginn asked.

"About three miles down the river road," Giles said.

"Then I need a ride," said Maginn. "The trolley doesn't go that far."

"Are you serious about this, Fitz?" Cadden asked. "That lovely woman really wants this clown to visit her in her rooms? At night?"

"She did seem excited."

"This is unbelievable," Cadden said.

"It's normal," Maginn said.

Maginn, at forty-nine, could not be called good-looking. His hairline had moved backward, his drooping gray mustache was ineptly darkened with mustache wax. He did not fit the lothario image, but his sensuality gave him an exotic appeal to many women. Why shouldn't the fireman's wife be one of his herd?

"I can take you down," Giles said, "but you'll have to find your own way back."

"Maybe I'll stay the week."

"Just be careful. Her husband's got a temper."

"Isn't he in Westchester?"

"That's what she said."

"Then why shouldn't we believe her?" Maginn asked. "What do you think, Edward?"

"I don't know what to think about you, Maginn. And I certainly don't know what to think about this woman. You're making a career out of intrigue."

Edward said he had a meeting but would drop by at Giles's house later to learn the outcome. Giles and Cadden drove Maginn to the house of assignation, which was dark.

"Doesn't look like anybody's home," Maginn said.

"You want us to wait?" Giles asked as Maginn stepped down onto the carriage drive.

"I'll go with him, make sure he gets in," Cadden said.

Maginn mounted the steps, knocked, won no response. He turned to Cadden, who stood in the moonlight at the bottom of the stoop, and shrugged, knocked louder. A light went on and Maginn smiled at Cadden.

"Who is it?" a voice from inside whispered.

"Is that you, Sally? It's Thomas Maginn, your admirer from the barge."

The door flew open and from interior shadows a male voice boomed, "So you're the one who's seeing my wife! Well, you've seen her for the last time, you home-wrecking son of a bitch!"

A man loomed from the shadows, pistol in hand, and fired two thunderclaps at Maginn, who was already on the run down the carriageway with Cadden.

"Hurry up, for God's sake," Cadden said.

"So there's two of you!" yelled the man with the gun, and he fired another shot. Cadden fell on his face and Maginn kept running, turned to see the man coming toward him, and clambered wildly into the carriage.

"He'll kill us all," Giles said, whipping the horse. And the carriage careened down the drive. Maginn looked back and saw the man pointing his gun at the inert Cadden.

"Christ," Maginn said, "that bastard shot Cadden for no reason. He's killed him. He's a lunatic!"

"Some men are like that about their wives," Giles said, urging the horse to a wild gallop.

"We should go back for Cadden," Maginn said.

"You want to get us shot too?"

"But he's hurt. We've got to call the cops."

"And tell them what?"

Maginn did not answer. They drove to Giles's town house and found Edward waiting, sipping whiskey in the drawing room. Maginn manically recounted the terror, the fall of plucky Cadden, incoherent flight, his desire to straighten things out. Edward listened with head-shaking sympathy.

"If Cadden is dead he's dead," Edward said. He paused for reflection. "If he's not dead he'll probably admit to that irate man what was happening. But if he mentions Giles's carriage, they'll come here looking for you."

Edward stood and paced.

"What you need is an alibi," he said to Maginn. "We'll go upstairs and get you into bed and if anybody comes we'll swear you've been here for hours."

"You'd do that?" Maginn asked Edward.

"What happened wasn't your fault, was it?"

"You think it'll work?"

"An alibi worked for those fellows who beat up the cops on the barge," Edward said. "And what choice do you have?"

"I'd get into that bed if I were you," Giles said. "We'll figure out what to do about Cadden. I'll get in touch with Sally. Here, have a drink."

He poured a whiskey for Maginn, who swallowed it in a gulp.

Giles led the way to an empty bedroom and lighted a lamp. Maginn sat on a chair and took off his clothes.

"Underwear too," Giles said. "If you're naked it's a better alibi. Am I right, Edward?"

"It's logical."

Giles handed the lamp to Edward, diminishing bedside light, then pulled down the covers so Maginn could crawl beneath them.

Cadden walked into the room.

"Aren't you in bed a little early, Maginn?" he asked.

Maginn by then had rolled fully under the covers and was lying in ten pounds of soggy gingersnaps that had been mixed with four quarts of warm chicken fat and spread between the sheets.

The puerile reduction of Maginn was a supreme success, but gave no satisfaction. It generated a predictable withdrawal in Maginn, but also in Edward, whose guilt was such that he stopped work on his new play, yet another confounding of intentions. Whatever seemed the right thing invariably proved otherwise. Could it be, Edward, that you were meant to be confounded unto the grave, that your destiny is linked to the everlastingly wrong choice? Was Katrina the wrong choice? Weren't you ambivalent about your *Stolen Cushion*, about *The Baron*? Hasn't Maginn made you doubt even *The Car Barns*? Is the play-in-progress a mistake? You're a mindless achiever, moving toward you know not what. "Edward Daugherty, a formless lump of matter, was born into this world yesterday for no known reason." Your sadness is a pose, Edward, your Weltschmerz sliced like liverwurst. You are different from everyone you know. You can't afford to consider Maginn's idea that all effort is a quest for the great cipher. You need a pair of spiritual spectacles to see things as they are. Understand this, Edward: you are still living your preamble.

DINNER AT THE DAUGHERTYS'

July 4, 1907

THE HEAT WORSENED. All screened windows of the parlors and dining room were open, all curtains and drapes tied back to the extreme; but the house was without a breeze. Dinner would be wretchedly uncomfortable and Edward was almost ready to take off his coat and tell Giles to do the same.

The women were another matter. Neither Felicity nor Katrina could easily shed a layer of clothing, nor were they likely to, whatever the degree; but then they were used to suffering for their plumage. Why do they do that to themselves? Edward decided he would wait for the missing guests before suggesting a dinner in shirtsleeves. Sweating through the city's hot spell, instead of spending the holiday week in the Adirondacks, was his choice: a chance to meet socially with Melissa Spencer, the young actress Maginn was bringing to dinner.

With great verve in projecting the volatility of young love, with a face that demanded one's attention, and a foxish smile that kept it, Melissa had taken Edward over when he saw her onstage; for she seemed the incarnation of the female lead of his new play. Suffer the heat for such gain.

And so he had begun this Independence Day holiday by taking Katrina to Washington Park for the morning band concert and reading of the Declaration of Independence, then lunch at Keeler's and out to the Woodlawn Park track to see Giles's trotter, My Own Love, foal of Gallant Warrior, the horse Edward had tried in vain to give to Katrina's father. He had given it, instead, after neither Katrina nor her mother would accept it, to Giles, who had won frequently with it for years, then put it to stud, and now was reaping second-generational benefits; today the foal won its heats and also tied a track record, 2:01 for the mile.

Edward poured sherry for the Fitzroys, a pony of very old port for Katrina, and a Scotch whisky and water for himself. They were all in the Daugherty drawing room, sitting near the windows to harvest the breeze, should it arrive, rubber plants and ferns in lush leaf among them. The room's personality reflected Katrina's devotion to the revered dead. Geraldine, Jacob, and Adelaide, in hanging portraits, and Katrina's poet, Baudelaire, in a pen-sketched self-portrait, all stared down at the occupants of the room. On a table between French porcelain vases and jade dragons the marble bust of the naked Persephone (a Katrina look-alike Edward had given her for their first anniversary) now seemed apt, chiefly as an adornment for the tomb of the Katrina-that-was: full woman then, now suitable only for admiration. Jacob Taylor's pendulum clock hung silently on the wall, permanently stopped at 8:53 to memorialize the approximate instant when the burning stick pierced Katrina's breast. And atilt on its hook opposite the mantel, a large gilt-framed mirror ensured that with even a cursory glance, one could monitor one's own or the collective image of this overheated quartet: all eyes, including her own, always on Katrina and her chamber of venerated memory, her sumptuous crypt of exhausted life.

"Maginn is late, as usual," Edward said.

"When we're gathered around his deathbed," said Giles, "he'll be someplace else."

"Do you have him to dinner often?" Felicity asked Katrina.

"Now and then. Why do you ask?"

"I find him so coarse, rather low-class in his tastes. And he paws you if he finds the opportunity."

"He's tried to get next to Felicity for years," Giles said, "hasn't he, love?"

"He has. It's quite obscene what he once said to me."

"Whatever did he say?" Katrina asked.

"I wouldn't repeat it."

"Paraphrase it," Edward said. "Give us a thrill."

"It had to do with anatomy," Felicity said. "Mine."

"And a splendid anatomy it is," said Giles.

"Maginn does like women," Edward said. "He's also tried his hand at Katrina."

"Not at all," Katrina said. "It's all talk."

"He went after you in our garden."

"No, no, no. He was flirting."

"What I saw was beyond flirting."

"We are never sure of what we see."

Edward let it go. She would forever deny the slightest dalliance. On Francis Phelan, she was vehement. Even Giles's pitiful effort at a beach picnic ("May I touch your naked shoulder?") she dismissed as an excess of friendship ("Just a lovable, silly man"). Like flies after sugar. The veneration of sugar.

"Maginn is afflicted, like a man with a stutter or a limp. He can't help it," Edward said.

"When God was handing out social graces," Giles said, "Maginn was elsewhere, trying to seduce an angel."

"Aren't angels sexless?" Felicity asked.

"That would merely present Maginn with a challenge," Edward said.

"But he's just a reporter, such a common person," Felicity said.

"I used to be a reporter," Edward said. "Is that your view of my social position?"

"You're very different."

"You really mustn't speak about people as 'common,'" Giles said. "You shouldn't type people that way."

"Not even if it's true?"

"It's snobbish. Not everybody has the good fortune to be born into money and social status."

"Are you quite sure that's good fortune?" Katrina said.

"Who is this woman he's bringing?" Felicity asked from her severe pout.

"Melissa Spencer, an actress," said Katrina.

"Oh dear," said Felicity. "Isn't 'actress' just another name for, you know . . ."

"Felicity," Giles said, "you have no idea who this young woman is. She's only eighteen and she's going to be in Edward's new play."

"Oh I am sorry," said Felicity.

"Don't waste your sorrow on Melissa," Edward said. "She's a very talented young lady. I saw her in a Sardou play in New York, and I knew if she toned down the melodramatics, she could act my heroine. She's at Proctor's this week in a comic opera, and so I sent her a script, and yesterday my producer came up from New York and we auditioned her. She was perfect—articulate, with an open heart, and a beauty that's hard to define. She commands one's attention."

"She certainly commands yours," Felicity said.

"Why shouldn't beauty be appreciated?" Katrina asked.

"It should, I suppose."

"It should be cast in bronze, carved in marble like Persephone there," said Giles, pointing to the marble bust. "Beauty is how we stay alive. It's why I married you, my love," and he patted Felicity's wrist.

"That's a ridiculous reason to marry, Giles," said Katrina. "I don't believe that's what drew you to Felicity."

"I swear it's true," said Giles.

"I doubt it. People want an unknown they can embrace. Something mysterious."

"Do you really think we're so anxious for the exotic?" Giles asked.

"But of course," Katrina said. "What else is love but the desire for prostitution?"

"Oh my," said Felicity. "You don't mean that."

"She means prostitution as a metaphor," Giles said.

"Not at all," said Katrina.

"I've been dying to ask what you've chosen for dinner," Felicity said. "I always love your menus."

"We start with prostitute soup," Katrina said.

"You do say the most outlandish things, Katrina," Felicity said. "You like to shock us."

"Do I? Is that true, Edward?"

"Offending people has always been one of the pleasures of the upper class," Edward said.

"I left the upper class when I married you," Katrina said.

"Perhaps you did," said Edward. "I remember Cornelia Wickham's saying I made you *declassée*. In spite of that, you certainly brought your elite social codes to the altar."

"Cornelia was jealous that Katrina was the true princess of Albany's social life," Giles said. "I remember her coming-out cotillion, the most elaborate the city had seen in decades. Cornelia looked radiant, and her dress, made by a London couturier who had gone on to design for the Queen, was the talk of the city. Yet every eye was on Katrina. All the men had to dance with her, including myself. The women, polite as they were, were wretchedly jealous, and it got into the social columns. Cornelia still hasn't forgiven her."

"Cornelia was a vain and brainless ninny," Katrina said. "I went to her cotillion determined to annoy her, and I flirted outrageously with everyone."

"You became the belle of someone else's ball," Giles said, "a mythic figure in society. And Cornelia married bountifully and grew fat as a toad."

"Is there something wrong in being fat?" Felicity asked.

"Nothing at all," Giles said. "After I lose interest in you, my dear, you may get as fat as you like."

"I will never be fat, Giles," Felicity said. "And it may be I who lose interest."

Footsteps on the porch announced that Maginn and Melissa had arrived.

At dinner, Maginn-by-candlelight looked less like Melissa's escort than somebody's ne'er-do-well uncle, with his waning, scraggly hair and mustache, expensive but wrinkled blue-silk tie, and his trademark coat with velvet collar: a coat for all seasons. His shirt collar was freshly starched, but only when Edward was sure he was wearing the complete shirt, and not just a dickey, did he give the word for the men to doff jackets. Edward and Giles, in their tailored shirts, ties in place, seemed aloof from the heat. Coatless, Maginn looked steamed.

Edward suggested the women could follow suit in whatever way feasible, and Melissa removed her diaphanous tunic, revealing shoulders bare except for where her light-brown hair fell onto them, and the string straps holding up her loose-fitting beige gown. It was clear she wore no corset, nor could Edward see any evidence of that new device, the brassiere. Her gown became the object of silent speculation: would it offer the table, before dinner's end, an unobstructed chest-scape?

"The play by Edward is so exciting," Melissa said. "I'm so flattered to be asked to even *read* for the role of Thisbe. There's such pathos in her. It's too good to be true, but it is true, isn't it, Edward?"

"We can't be sure about anything," Edward said, "but you will have the part if we're not all stricken by disaster."

"There's always the odd chance," Maginn said, "that the play will be a disaster."

"Oh no," said Melissa. "It's a wonderful play."

"That has nothing to do with it," Maginn said.

"Here now," said Giles, "let's not have any sour grapes."

"Maginn is right," Edward said. "Even great plays, and I make no argument for my own, are often badly received. *The Seagull* was mocked in its St. Petersburg premiere, and this year a horde of benighted Irishmen rioted at the Abbey Theatre over Synge's language in *Playboy of the Western World*."

"I won't hear of any disasters," Melissa said. "Have you read Edward's play, Mrs. Daugherty?"

"Of course. It was enthralling."

"I agree. It's gotten even better as I commit it to memory."

"You've memorized it already?" asked Katrina.

"Rather a lot of it," Melissa said. "Actors must read a play countless times, although I know some who memorize only their own lines and cues."

"Some do even less," Katrina said. "They bumble through and think it enough just to stand there and shimmer in the footlights. Have you known actresses who only shimmer?"

"I've only been in theater a year," Melissa said, and she turned to Felicity. "Does theater thrill you as it does me?"

"I rarely go," Felicity said. "In New York I went once and found it extremely improper. Women in tights, that sort of thing."

"Felicity is easily shocked," Giles said.

"I saw Edward's last play," Felicity said, "but I didn't entirely understand it."

"What didn't you understand?" Melissa asked.

"The words," Maginn said.

"The play has a political theme," said Giles, "and my wife doesn't understand politics, do you, my love?"

"I'm not a simp, Giles."

"Let Felicity speak for herself, Giles," Katrina said. "Don't be such a mother hen."

"Those pearls you're wearing are gorgeous," Melissa said to Felicity. "I've never seen anything like them."

"Giles gave them to me for our anniversary."

"And your hair," said Melissa. "I wish I had such beautiful hair."

"How nice of you to say that," said Felicity. "Your own hair is very lovely. I'm sure you shimmer beautifully onstage, and I'll bet you don't forget your lines."

Edward saw Felicity as not unattractive, a hint of the hoyden in her manner, and with a flouncy appeal, undergirded by that heralded anatomy. Her hair, a mass of thick black waves, loosely plaited and gathered in soft coils to just below her shoulders, was truly beautiful, but neither bronze nor marble could rescue her long nose and small eyes. Edward also decided Melissa was extremely shrewd, with the good sense to back off an argument about acting with Katrina, and with instant insight as to where Felicity was most susceptible to flattery.

Loretta came to take the soup bowls and Katrina introduced her to the table as "Loretta McNally, just here from Ireland. Cora's youngest sister. Lovely Cora who died in the Delavan. Loretta isn't a servant. She's like family."

Katrina: reconstituting Cora through her sibling, replaying the psychic games she invented for that bygone girl: taking Cora to tea at the homes of social friends, teaching her how to sit a horse, and the names of flowers and jewels, correcting her posture, her speech, coiffing her hair, giving her clothes, lifting Cora up from Irish peasantry into Katrina's own shining world.

"You're arousing expectations that can't be fulfilled," Edward had argued.

"Nonsense. When she knows how to move she'll rise."

"All she'll have is a mask of pretense."

"Then she'll be like everybody else."

And which mask are you wearing tonight, Katrina? Princess of the social elite? Benefactor of proles? Beloved of cats? Iconic prostitute before her mirror?

Loretta was serving individual silver bowls of cold crabmeat on beds of cracked ice, with the pale-green sauce Edward recognized as his mother's, created for the Patroon's table. Katrina, knowing the sauce pleased Edward's palate, learned the recipe from Hanorah, then saw to it her own cook, Mrs. Squires, made it to Edward's satisfaction.

"Let's go back to your play, Edward," Maginn said. "Why did you write it? I find its structure extremely strange."

"You've read it?"

"I borrowed Melissa's copy last night."

Edward looked at Melissa, whose eyes were on the crabmeat. "That wasn't for circulation," he said.

"I cajoled her," Maginn said. "I told her we were very old friends. I told her I was best man at your wedding and you wouldn't mind. I know you've been working on it for years. Was it a major problem, getting the form?"

"It took the necessary time," Edward said. "You can't rush it. When the matter is ready the form will come."

"I prefer to think that when the form is ready the matter will come," Maginn said.

"I was echoing Aristotle. Your remark is pure Oscar Wilde."

"There is no pure Oscar Wilde," said Maginn.

"You don't like my play?"

"It's so ethereal," said Maginn. "Where's your trademark realism? Or those cherished political themes?"

"I left all that out."

"But without that the play flies off into myth, and artsy romanticism."

"You faulted *The Car Barns* for being *too* political. 'Radical art,' you called it. Now, with no radicalism, I'm artsy. I can't find a happy medium with you, Maginn."

"What is this play about?" Giles asked.

"It's a somber love story," Melissa said. "Beautiful and very romantic."

"But what is it about?"

"It starts from the myth of Pyramus and Thisbe, Ovid's version," Edward said. "Two lovers, kept apart by their families, find a way to meet. Thisbe arrives by the light of the moon, sees a lioness who has just finished a kill and has come to drink at a fountain near the tomb where she is to meet Pyramus. Thisbe drops her veil and flees, the lioness finds the veil, mauls it with bloody paws and jowls, and leaves. Pyramus arrives, finds the bloody veil, and assumes Thisbe has been killed. Disconsolate, he kills himself with his sword. Thisbe emerges from hiding, finds her lover dying, and also kills herself. That's the myth. I alter it considerably. No lioness, no sword."

"But it's so fated," said Maginn, "all wrapped up in God's intellect. God is mindless, Edward, don't you know that? The random moment is what's important, not the hounds of fate. It's time we left Oedipus behind. We should be our own gods, not their pawns. I believe in whim, not wisdom."

"Your random moment," Edward said, "means to live like a blown leaf. I do believe in impulses, but I believe they come from something central to what we are, that they're signals for action—a craving for sacrifice in exchange for love, an instinct for evil we can't escape. We're mostly ignorant of what's really going on in our souls, but we should give the signals a chance."

"Instinct for evil," Maginn said. "You sound like a Catholic missionary saving heathens from original sin."

"And you," said Katrina, "sound like a misanthrope. What ever pleases you, Thomas?"

"You please me, Katrina, the way you please the world. I'm overcome with pleasure when I see beauty and wit come together. And I value our visiting Miss Melissa, a young woman with a future. I do have my moments, and they arrive quite randomly."

"I remember one of your random moments," said Giles. "Your date with the fireman's wife."

"You never forget that, do you, Fitz?"

"That was so funny," said Felicity.

"Depending on your perspective," said Maginn.

"Who is the fireman's wife?" Melissa asked.

"An invention of these grown-up boys," said Katrina, pointing to Edward and Giles.

"Consummate actors, both," Maginn said. "They set out to humiliate me and they did it extremely well."

"Humiliation wasn't the intention," Giles said. "It was a joke. If we weren't close friends we wouldn't have bothered."

"They took advantage of Thomas's infatuation with Felicity's aunt," Katrina said, "and convinced him she felt the same way."

"I told my aunt all about it," Felicity said. "She was amused and flattered, but she'd never cheat on her husband."

"An exceedingly rare woman," said Maginn. "Almost extinct in our time."

"Oh, you are a wretched man," Katrina said.

"Hateful," said Felicity. "Devilish."

"You know what Chaucer said, my dears. 'One shouldn't be too inquisitive in life either about God's secrets or one's wife.' Do you hear what I'm saying about God, Edward?"

"I do hear," Edward said.

"*Mundus vult decipi,*" said Giles.

"What's that again?" Edward asked.

"The world wants to be deceived," Giles said. "Don't you think so?"

"What happened with the fireman's wife?" Melissa asked.

"When Thomas went to meet her," Giles said, "a jealous husband shot at him and he fled for his life. The husband was played by a friend of ours, Clubber Dooley. He screamed at Maginn as a home-wrecker and fired blank cartridges. Grand melodrama, a high point of Clubber's life."

"Dooley is pitiful," Maginn said.

"I wouldn't say so," said Giles.

"He drinks in Johnny Groelz's saloon, morose, all but toothless, swilling beer till he's senseless. Once a week a boy comes in and Dooley hands him money and the boy takes it home to Mother, a slattern who once indulged Dooley—what way, precisely, I'd rather develop bubonic plague than try to imagine. But ever since then she's been on dreadful Dooley's dole, and he dreams of another go at her someday, if he can only find a way to get off the barstool. Pitiful, needy sap."

"That's perverse," said Giles. "That boy is related to Clubber. His mother raised Clubber."

"Intimacy within the family is not a new thing in the universe," Maginn said.

"Always sex," said Katrina. "Thomas the satyr, eternally pursuing the nymphs."

"The Greeks made bucolic gods of the satyrs," Maginn said, "and I find it a jovial way of life, bouncing through the bosky with divine goatishness, spying one's pleasure, taking it, then moving on to the next pasture. Is there a better way to spend one's day?"

"You are moving into depravity," Katrina said.

Edward saw she was smiling.

Loretta appeared at Katrina's elbow to say dessert was ready, and Katrina announced it would be served on the back piazza, with fireworks to follow.

Edward had put his son in charge of the fireworks, and now here he came: Martin Daugherty, twenty, home from his day's wandering. He stepped onto the piazza carrying his dish of Mrs. Squires's ice cream, looking, Edward thought, like himself at that age: tall, with abundant brown hair all in place, still not quite grown into his teeth, wearing a fresh white shirt with cuffs turned. Edward saw Martin's eyes go directly to Melissa.

"This is our son, Martin," Edward said. Martin stopped at Melissa's chair and took her hand in greeting. "Melissa Spencer." And they smiled. Both of an age.

"You look like your father," Melissa said. "A handsome family indeed."

A beginning? Two beginnings?

"Melissa will play the lead in my new play, all things being equal," Edward said.

"That's exciting," Martin said. "A pleasure, Miss Spencer."

"All things are never equal, Edward," Maginn said. "You should avoid inaccurate clichés."

"Are you in school?" Melissa asked Martin.

"Going into my third year at Fordham."

"He may be a writer like his father," Katrina said. "He writes well."

"No, not like my father. I'm not serious about it."

"It takes time to be serious," Katrina said. "He's a fine student."

"I might write for the newspapers," Martin said.

"That's such an exciting world," Melissa said.

"It's about as exciting," said Maginn, "as being attacked by fleas."

"Are you really so bored by your work, Maginn?" Edward asked.

"I would infinitely prefer setting off fireworks as a way of life," Maginn said.

"I just came from the fireworks at Beaver Park," Martin said. "A huge crowd. A horse ran wild when somebody threw a cannon cracker at him. He was pulling an Italian peddler's vegetable wagon and he ran into a moving trolley. He was on his side and bleeding badly, two legs obviously broken."

"Oh that's awful," said Melissa, and she hid her face in her hands.

"The peddler kept asking the policeman to shoot the horse, but the cop said he couldn't kill an animal like that."

"You have to, if they're in that condition," Giles said. "You have to shoot them."

"A man came out of a house with a rifle and said he'd shoot the horse. The Italian got down on his knees and begged him to do it, and the man shot the horse in the head."

"Horrible," said Melissa, and she wept for the horse.

"I also saw Jack Apple do his annual jump into the river," Martin said, breaking a silence. "He jumped off the top of the Maiden Lane bridge."

"He only jumped *off* it?" Giles said. "Anybody can do that. The trick is to jump *over* it."

"Oh Giles," Felicity said.

"Giles is warming up his jokes," Maginn said. "Edward, have you considered casting Giles as Pyramus in your play? You'd have them tumbling out of their seats. Or rolling in the aisles, as you might put it."

"The fireworks are in those bags at the foot of the steps," Edward said.

Martin inspected the skyrockets, Roman candles, flowerpots, cherry bombs, strings of Chinese crackers; and Edward watched the women as they watched each other, a study in optics: Katrina aware of Giles's and Felicity's fascination with Melissa's unblushing attitude toward her body; Melissa aware of Edward's eyes on her, her own eyes on Katrina, evaluating. Edward monitored the shifting glance, the recurrent stare that extended an instant too long to be insignificant. He observed Maginn giving equal attention to all three women: failed with Felicity, failed with Katrina—didn't he? Will he fail with Melissa, or does she collect men as he collects women? Her smiling eye lingered on Edward an instant too long not to be significant. Edward saw that Maginn saw.

The fireworks sizzled, glowed, exploded with great bangs and a thousand small, oriental poppings, and the Roman candles thupthupped toward where the lawn sloped down toward the brickyard on Van Woert Street, all this under Martin's expert hand. Edward had taken him to see fireworks the first year of his life and ever after taught him caution in their handling.

"I suppose all over Albany right now," Edward said, "boys are having their fingers blown off and their eyes blown out."

"Giles, how come you're not with the firemen tonight?" Maginn asked. "Don't you usually help them out on the Fourth?"

"I took the night off to have dinner with you, you lout," Giles said. "I'm tired of stupid people blowing themselves to pieces. But if you decide to blow yourself up, Maginn, I have the tetanus antitoxin in my bag to treat you."

"If I decide to blow myself up," said Maginn, "there won't be anything left to treat. I will very thoroughly atomize myself into the circumambient air."

"What a grisly thing to say," Katrina said.

"Grisly? I thought it was quite poetic. You're very severe with me tonight, Katrina."

Grisly the whole thing. And unacceptable. Edward rose from his rocker and walked down onto the lawn to get away. Something magnetic in him attracts her lashing tongue. Of course she knows he lives for these lashings. What is the recourse?

"Time for the skyrockets," Martin said.

"Oooh, can I light one?" Melissa asked, and she left the piazza and came to the bottom of the garden, where Edward and Martin stood beside a dozen skyrockets stuck into the ground on their launching sticks. Martin handed her the lighted punk and showed her where to touch it to a skyrocket's fuse. She bent over the sky-rocket, very probably giving Martin an unobstructed view of the chest-scape; and, as they all watched the rocket ignite, soar into the moonlit sky, and explode, Melissa touched another rocket, then another, sending them all to heaven. From the piazza came applause for the spectacle.

As Edward and Melissa walked back toward the house she touched his arm. He turned to see her leaning toward him, offering him her beautiful moonlit breasts.

"I just wanted to say I'm incredibly grateful for your belief in me," she said. "You're a very special man."

"I recognize talent when I see it," Edward said. He offered her his hand and they went up the steps together.

Maginn rose from his chair and came over to Edward.

"Are you taking her away from me?" he whispered. "Is that what you're doing?"

Before Edward could answer, Felicity said, "Look, a shooting star!" and he turned to see in the northern sky the dying arc of the meteor, or was it a comet, or a falling angel?

"Oh dear," Melissa said, blessing herself. "That's bad luck. That means one of us here will be dead next year."

"More fatalism, Edward," Maginn said. "This superstitious child is perfect for your play."

"I don't believe such things," Katrina said.

"On the other hand, the Trojans didn't believe Cassandra's prophecies," Maginn said, "and look what happened to them."

"We're all too healthy to die," Felicity said.

"I agree," Edward said. "I refuse to play dead just because the sky is falling."

"I second that motion," said Giles.

At the stroke of midnight Martin lit the last fireworks of the evening: half a dozen red lights that burned brightly together for a long minute at the bottom of the garden, then weakened until their lambency was spent, and the light on the Daugherty lawn came only from the vigilant moon.

THE RAPE OF FELICITY:
TWO VERSIONS

EDWARD: FROM THE INQUEST REPORT

SHE WAS THERE when I came into the apartment, wearing that exotic cloak and mask, moving nervously around the parlor, and exploding with her story. She said she was napping on the sofa in her room, fully dressed, when she saw a man crawling over the transom, half into the room through the fanlight's opening; and what awakened her was the sound of his shirt buttons scraping on the wood.

"I would have screamed," she said, "but he waved a knife at me in silent warning. I ran to the buzzer to ring for help, but he was at me before I got to it, and he searched my purse and valise. He took all the cash I'd drawn from the bank in Albany, more than three hundred dollars, and he touched the long strand of pearls I was wearing, the ones Giles gave me. He seemed to know jewelry. 'Now,' he said to me, 'get out of your clothes.'"

She wept as she said this, lifting her eye mask to dab

at her tears. I asked her why she was wearing the mask but she just waved both hands impatiently.

"He led me to the bedroom and pushed me onto the bed and raped me, hurt me so much I thought I must be bleeding. When he was done he made me draw water for a bath and told me to sit in the water and soap myself. He knelt by the tub and lathered me with one hand, his knife always at me. He helped me out of the tub and handed me a towel to dry off, then opened the wardrobe and took out this mask and cloak. I never saw them before and can't imagine how he knew they were there. Maybe he'd put them there.

"He told me, 'Lady, you got one great shape,' and made me put on the mask, cloak, and shoes and walk across the room, holding the cloak open while he looked at me. Then he pushed me down on the sofa and raped me again. And he left. I knew you [me] had an apartment here, and this morning I saw Melissa in the lobby and I assumed she was visiting you. So when he was gone I grabbed my clothes and came straight here, afraid he'd come back for another go at me, or even kill me, that's how these men are. Oh the foul dog."

Melissa told me she was shocked to see a masked woman at the door, and wasn't sure it was Felicity until she spoke. Felicity's arrival was a quarter hour before my own, and all that time, Melissa said, she was hysterical, talking of being raped and robbed of her money and pearls by a man she'd seen working in the hotel. When I arrived Felicity told me the rapist looked like one of the gang who beat up the policemen on the barge. When she described him I knew it was Cully Watson. Melissa knew Cully only as Hopkins, a sometime hotel elevator operator.

Melissa, Felicity, and I were together half an hour, sifting what had happened, when Giles arrived. Never has a man been more deceived about what he thought he was seeing. Such costly, ghastly error. The questions remain: What led to his insane behavior? How did he know Felicity would be in my room at that moment, when neither we nor Felicity could have predicted it?

CULLY WATSON: FROM HIS STATEMENT TO POLICE

I was in Ohio first I heard of those killings. It was the Doc's wife and the actress, and Daugherty. Something going on there. Same day as the killings a guy says the Albany cops are looking for me, want me for trial, so what I needed was a bundle to get gone. The Doc's wife liked me, so when I took her stuff up to her room I patted her on the ass. She opened her bag to duke me and I saw a fold of bills thick as a steak. I told her, "I don't want money, just a little lovin'." I already had her three times before when she was at the hotel, so I muzzled her up. Not now, somebody's comin' to see me, she said. I said I'll be quick, and I opened her up some and she let me do this and that but pushed me away.

"We'll do it all later," she said, but I'm hot so I kept going and we did it on the davenport.

She liked it but she was pissed at me mussing her hair, she's got company coming. Then the door opened and in came the actress. She didn't know what to make of us, both half naked, and she backed out, but the Doc's wife said, "He's raping me, don't go."

I said, "No, I'm just fucking her. We're friends." And I pulled out of her.

"I wanna take a bath," the Doc's wife said, and she turned on the tap in the tub, bare-ass, except for that long string of pearls. I told her I liked the way she looked in 'em so she took 'em off to spite me and threw 'em on the bed. They said I took 'em but that ain't so. Fencing jewels on the run, you gotta be stupid. The other woman kept looking at me and she wasn't afraid.

"Are you busy?" I said.

"Forget it," she said.

"Maybe you wanna take a bath too."

"No thanks," she said, but I pulled her clothes off. She

fought me pretty good, but I got it into her too, short time, just to say I did it, a hell of a sweet-looking bitch. I put 'em both in the tub, soaping each other up. I coulda diddled the two of 'em all day, but with the cops after me I slipped out, took the cash from the purse, and left the women playing foot-in-the-crotch. I don't know who was doing what to who in that crowd. Maybe everybody was doing everybody. For me, I was long gone before the killings. When I heard about them I didn't blame the Doc. His wife was no good. But she was a pretty good fuck.

EDWARD VISITS A MOVIE SET

June 10, 1910

MISS INNOCENCE OF America. If a headbirth by Aphrodite and The Prince were possible she could have been the progeny: born with passion's mouth and sacred swath, and wisdom from below. There are lessons to be learned by brushing a wing against such as she, and the lessons continue. In Melissa's nest of tinder I remembered Rose from tent city: vivacious, talented, driven, exuberant, bright, cunning strumpet. She answered when I wrote that I wanted to talk about Felicity.

> *Can you remember the dress I wore when we met? It no longer fits me, I'm so thin. The Kinegraph people think I'm ill or dying. They even say it to my face. I still wake up calling your name over and over. You've never left me. Some weeks I hardly eat anything. I'm wasting away, they tell me, and you know an actress can't afford to lose her profile.*

Sickness plagues her imagination. She falls mortally ill when life goes awry, when fortune balks, when love loses its luminescence; for if you are ill, God cannot refuse you sustenance. It was because I genuinely believed her inability to either sleep without night sweats, or draw breath without pain, that I was with her when death came at us out of Giles's pistol. She and I were finished, but I had been unable to reject that face: not beautiful, but so robustly young, and illusory. Believe that face and lose your way. Study the transformation as she applies the powders, rouges, and charcoal stripings. Discover in that colored mouth, in those magnified eyes, the lure of the virgin-into-vixen: kill my innocence and I'll reward you with my fur.

I've made thirty-five films this year and until two months ago nobody knew my name. And I thought I'd be anonymous forever. Of course I'd love to see you. Always. I was supposed to make two films last week and I missed both because of my weakness, but now that we're leaving the city I'm wonderfully well, for we're going to a marvelous lake with wild woodland. Do you know where I'm talking about? I can't believe it. I'm so excited. I told them everything I knew about the place, and my director couldn't wait. We'll be at our hotel four weeks, so come, love, please come, and everything will be just as it was.

Her success as my Thisbe had been supreme, she famous overnight, her photo in all the magazines. The play ran five months and when it closed Flo Ziegfeld was ready to put her in his *Miss Innocence* to replace Anna Held, but along came Giles's Wild West performance and Ziegfeld said nobody tainted by scandal would ever be in a show of his. For a time no one in theater would hire her, but the scandal faded into gossip and instead of being branded as the vixen she emerged as destiny's waif, the innocent darling corrupted by the "eater of broken meats," as the *Police Gazette* labeled me.

She sought work in the pictures, brought her photographs to Kinegraph, and was hired at fifteen dollars a week. Her salary rose to six hundred a week and is still climbing. She's become Kinegraph's chief asset: The Kinegraph Girl, nameless, chameleonic face of sorrow and rapture and fury and terror and wickedness and determination and invitation.

During one of her illnesses rumors spread that she'd been killed by a burglar, or run down by a drunken motorist. The public wondered: Where has our girl gone? Kinegraph publicists advertised in the newspapers to disprove the lies about her death, and announced she was coming to New York for a new picture. Squadrons of police had to hold back fans waiting for her train at Grand Central—a greater crowd than greeted the President the previous week. Kinegraph promptly abandoned its policy of anonymity for actors and agreed the public should know the Kinegraph Girl by name: Melissa Spencer . . . Melisssssssssa Sssssssssspencccccccer, how sweet the sibilance!

> *My sickness flared up when the police came to talk about Cully Watson. All lies. How can such a man be believed? If they put it in the papers again my career is ruined. Why would he slander me? I never said a word to him, and I swear this on my breasts, which you know how much we both value. Please meet me at Cooperstown and we will erase the horror and relive our loving days there and I'll be well again just from the sight of you.*

Her film-in-progress was *The Deerslayer*, Cooper's five-hundred-page Natty Bumppo novel condensed to a twenty-minute movie. Her role was Hetty, the simpleminded daughter of scalp hunter Thomas Hutter. When I found my way to the village and then to the set, there she was, Melissa-into-Hetty, lying on her bed beneath a quilt, her face powdered into a death pallor; for Hetty had been shot by a stray bullet as the British troops rescued Deerslayer and Hetty's sister, Judith, from torture at the hands of the Huron Indians. Hetty was dying, and her secret love, Hurry Harry, another scalp hunter, was by her deathbed, along with Judith, heroic Deerslayer in his fringed buckskins, and his bare-chested Indian friend Chingachgook, noble Delaware chief. The actors mouthed Cooper's cumbersome dialogue as if it meant something to the film.

"How come they to shoot a poor girl like me and let so many men go unharmed?" Hetty wondered.

" 'Twas an accident, poor Hetty," said Judith.

"I'm glad of that—I thought it strange: I am feebleminded, and the red men have never harmed me before . . . there's something the matter with my eyes—you look dim and distant—and so does Hurry, now I look at him . . . my mind was feeble—what people call half-witted . . . How dark it's becoming! . . . I feel, Deerslayer, though I couldn't tell you why . . . that you and I are not going to part forever . . ."

". . . Yes, we *shall* meet ag'in, though it may be a long time first and in a far-distant land."

"Sister, where are you? I can't see now anything but darkness . . ."

"Speak, dearest," said Judith. "Is there anything you wish to say . . . in this awful moment?"

Cooper has Hetty blush, which to Judith means Hetty is undergoing "a sort of secret yielding to the instincts of nature," and, on cue from Judith, Hurry Harry, nature's lusty pawn, takes Hetty in his arms. She utters her love for him, then dies.

Melissa, no stranger at death's door, rose up from Hetty's bed twice, fell back twice to die twice, one of the film's notable scenes. When it ended and the camera ceased its clatter, she rose up again to embrace me, kiss me lightly but with promise. The director eyed our kiss with disapproval, and I sensed he was Melissa's new conquest. He was early thirtyish, boyish, and rumpled.

"Our next film's in California, where we'll never have to worry about the weather," he said. "And it gets us away from the patent wars—movie companies suing each other over who owns the camera technology. You know about that, I guess."

"Of course," I said, knowing nothing of such wars.

"Melissa has no interest in these things," said the rumpled boy, "but she'll thrive in California. Inspiration under the sun. You'll have that every day, Mel."

"A life of sunshine," Melissa said. "What luxury."

When Rumples ended the day's filming, Melissa changed clothes, leaving Hetty's shroud and heavy eye makeup behind, converting that face that launched a thousand nickels (ten thousand thousand nickels) back into its faux pristinity. We went to the hotel and found our way to the rear piazza with its same rockers, same hammock, same view of the lovely lake that Cooper called Glimmerglass, and its vast, lush forests. Here we had spent ten idyllic days in the summer of 1908, convinced life was a dream of sensual indolence.

Melissa took up her familiar position in the hammock, and we ordered the same drinks (gin and quinine water), set them on the same wicker table, and we studied each other as if the 1908 dream had not dissolved in cordite reek and blood spew. Two years gone and the residual bone pain from the bullet (which had entered my left chest where the burning stick pierced Katrina: God's own symmetry) continued to plague my sleepless nights. Yet it was the forgotten wound, spoken of by neither Katrina nor Melissa; for I'd behaved badly, had not summoned the penitential grace to die from my bullet.

"Tell me about your play," she said. "Am I in it?"

"Someone like you is in it, but it isn't you."

"But I could play the role."

"You could if I cast you."

"Of course you'll cast me."

"Maybe you won't want this role."

"If you wrote it I want it."

"That's your only interest, a role. You don't even know what the play is about."

"What *is* it about?"

"It's about a marriage that fails and the partners stay together but take lovers, not very original. Then the husband is caught with his mistress in a love nest, there's a shooting and two die. The husband is shot but doesn't die. People wish he had. He is condemned as a lecherous cad by priests, newspaper editors, and other custodians of the high moral ground. His son abandons college to escape his father's scandal. Thoughtless of the father not to perish from shame. To spite others, the man lives on. His life grows bleak. He can't understand why this tragedy happened, why people died. It's a mystery. He begins a journal, fills ledgers with ruminations, theories, then decides writing a play will combat the lethal determinism of the universe. He fills his imagined stage with a riot of scenes that synthesize events, discover answers. He discovers little and falls depressed at the pointlessness of wild endeavor. In time he humbleheartedly reunites with his estranged wife as a way of saving his soul. Magnanimous woman, she doesn't loathe him. She has her own sorrows. She has always loved him and he her. This is such a commonplace story. It happens to everybody, don't you think? Finally, as he's framing a conclusion on the cause of the killings, he turns up facts that dramatically contradict his conclusion, so he vis-

its his old paramour to confront her with the news. That's as far as
I've gotten."

"When he goes back to his wife, do they make love?"

"I haven't decided if love is what they make."

"But they do sexual things."

"I haven't decided if what they do is sexual."

"You've forgotten what's sexual?"

"Not at all."

"Do you remember me making myself sexual in this hammock?"

"I do."

"Shall I do it again?"

She was nuding herself belowskirts. She could do this expedi-
tiously.

"Is anybody watching?"

"I am."

"I mean others."

"No."

"Is anybody coming?"

"No."

"You see how I still love you?"

"I see the contour of a sunrise."

"Shall we go to the room?"

"If you like."

"You're not enticed."

"I seem to be."

"Then say it."

"The room. Yes."

We went to her rustic chamber: bed, dresser, commode, basin
and pitcher, wallpaper with pink roses on a field of mattress ticking.
We shed our garments and I remembered vividly what I felt whenever I took this journey; but I felt none of that now, could not
invest my movement with the pelvic arrhythmia she would remember, if she could differentiate mine from others. She perceived the
problem and initiated variations on the theme, but while I remained
full-blooded, I did so with ice in my heart.

"You're like a hanged man," she said. "Erect but dead."

"I *am* a hanged man. At the end of my rope."

"You don't look dead. You look wonderful. You look like the man I fell in love with at your dinner party."

"That man is dead. Did you fall in love with your director? And what would he say if he saw you now?"

She was, just then, a moving picture, stirring the air with my verticality as if it were the tiller of a boat in a rowdy sea. My question becalmed her.

"Ah, you're jealous. How silly."

She always viewed my objection to her flirtations as the fettering of her soul.

"He knows about us," she said, "but he assumes we're a thing of the past."

"Would this scene convince him otherwise?"

"He's not important to me the way you are, and he's not very good at this." She jostled the tiller. "I told him we had a legal matter to discuss."

"And so we do."

"Not now."

She went to the dresser and found a long strand of pearls, put it around her neck and knotted it so the knot lay in the deep fallaway of her breasts. She straddled the tiller and let the pearls caress my chest, my face.

"Those look like Felicity's pearls," I said, and she reacted as if I'd lashed her with a bullwhip.

"Why would you say such a thing?" She knelt up straight, then put one foot on the floor, so beautiful in her angularity, her pudendal equipoise. "You think I stole them?"

"Cully Watson says he didn't take them, yet they did vanish. Odd he admits the money but denies the pearls."

"Maybe the police stole them. What do I care? How could you think I took them?"

"I never saw you wear pearls like these before."

"I loved Felicity's pearls, so I got my own."

"Saved your pennies, did you? Giles paid five thousand dollars for Felicity's."

"Mine were a gift from an extremely wealthy gentleman. You're being rotten."

"Cully contradicts everything you and Felicity told me."

"Cully!" she screamed. "I'm sick of Cully. He's a murderer. You take his word over mine?"

"Have you seen his statement?"

"Yes, and he's a maniac. It's all lies. ALL LIES! *ALL LIES!*"

She was kneeling on a pillow. She stood up, grabbed the pillow, and threw it at me.

"You son of a bitch, you believe him, don't you! You think I had sex with him! You think I was in the bathtub with Felicity! *YOU'RE A MANIAC TOO IF YOU BELIEVE THAT!*"

She threw a box of body powder at me. It missed my head, hit the wall, and showered talcum over the bedclothes. She reached for the toilet water but I wrapped her fury in a bear hug and made her put it down.

"That cape Felicity wore," I said. "I found the costumier where you bought it. I saw a similar cloak in his display window. He remembered you."

Her body went limp in my arms. I eased her backward so she could sit on the bed, and she blanched, summoning a stroke, or the black plague, anything to solve this crisis of contradiction. She buried her face in her hands as she had when she wept for the dead horse on the Fourth of July.

"You don't know anything," she said.

"I agree with that. Why don't you enlighten me?"

She fell backward on the bed and stretched her arms over her head, eyes closed, her cave of opulent nuances assisting her in negotiating a new reality.

"I gave Felicity the mask and cloak to wear for you."

"For me?"

"She wanted you. Wanted to be with you."

"Felicity wanted *me*?"

"For years. She could never tell you."

"Did it occur to her I might not want her?"

"You'd have wanted her if you saw her in that cloak."

"I did see her in it. Alive and dead."

"She had a beautiful body and she wanted to give it to you. I thought you'd like that. I said I'd arrange it. We made a game of how we'd both dress up for you."

"You never mentioned such a thing."

"It was new. We talked about it the week before. We wanted to surprise you."

"But Cully was the surprise."

"Yes."

"And he, not I, put you both in the tub."

"*NEVER!*"

She fumed in silence, stoking herself for an explosion of logic that would defy all argument. I pacified her with gin and in the ensuing half hour she cobbled together her story.

She bought the cloak for Felicity a week before the famous day, she said, kept it in a closet in our apartment (*ours* for the previous two months; but we were finished, for I'd wearied of her feigned illnesses, her absurd jealousies—over an actress who smiled at me at the theater, or a buxom waitress where we breakfasted—and her rage over these imagined dalliances. That rage would end as irrationally as it had begun: she on her knees asking forgiveness, I touching away her tears and reaffirming my loyalty with prolonged vaginal stroking). Melissa, having seen Felicity arrive in the hotel that morning, took cloak and mask to Felicity's room, the proposed site of our ménage. She put the garments on a chair but saw no Felicity; nor was she in the bedroom. Melissa called out, "Your wardrobe mistress has arrived," and from the bathroom came male and female voices, then Felicity's voice saying she would see Melissa later.

"I left immediately," Melissa said to me, "telling myself she was always something of a tart."

"You didn't hear any fear in her voice?"

"I suppose I should have."

"Wasn't that the bathtub rape in progress?"

"*If* he raped her. He said he raped me too, but I never set eyes on the man."

"You never told me any of this."

"She came to our door in that cloak, crying and carrying her clothes, hiding behind that mask. She cried rape and I let her in. She lied to you about the cloak, but how could she tell you what it was really for? Maybe she still hoped to charm you with it. Tarts are tarts. And yet how could I doubt her? She said he held a knife to her throat, that she even feared for *my* life when I was outside that bathroom door. I couldn't tell you this."

"Not even after her death, to get at the truth?"

"This is the truth!"

Melissa stood up and began to dress herself and I too stepped into my clothing, told her I was going back to Albany.

"You make it quite credible," I said. "I don't doubt any part of your story. But I'm absolutely certain you're a virtuoso liar."

KATRINA'S DIARY AND THE
BOVINE POEM

June 11, 1910

EDWARD ENTERED HIS home and from the hallway he called Katrina. The house replied with a stillness that plummeted him into gloom. He tossed his coat and hat on a chair and went to his library where Katrina would have left him a message, if she had been in a mood to communicate. He saw the letter from Melissa to Katrina, which lay unopened on his desk where Katrina had left it, along with two volumes of her diary for the years 1894 and 1908, their marking sashes emerging, presumably, from pages to be heeded. He pushed Melissa's letter aside and opened the pages of Katrina's mind.

The first diary: April 19, 1894
Mother sold her emerald last month. I've only now learned this. The house was in jeopardy and the emerald preserved it for at least four years. Father had far less than he let on, lost almost half a million in the panic of '93, and gave more than anyone knew to Madame Baldwin. He came to Mother with his problem. Had he not given her the jewels? Were they not emblematic of lush times? But now, after the panic, the times have us in a

precarious position. He did not mention Madame Baldwin. Mother yielded the emerald and kept his secrets, shoring up the facade of normalcy by forgoing travel to London and Paris for the year, limiting her shopping, and letting two of the lesser servants go. Of her truly valuable jewels only her black pearls and solitaire earrings remain, and, of course, her priceless tiara, which I covet.

Mother chaired her antisuffrage meeting today in our main parlor. Giles came, unable to resist Mother's magnetism. Edward brought me, listened for ten minutes, amused, then left for the club. The room was filled with a hundred of Mother's friends and peers, all so well educated, so certain of their position, so unified and uniformed in their spring bonnets against the amendment that would eliminate the word "male" from the State Constitution's definition of suffrage. Mother was valiant, insisting an undesirable class of women would swiftly take advantage of the vote, that it is a man's sphere for which women are unsuited. Could anyone, she inquired in her shrillest tone, imagine a proper woman serving in the militia, or on the police and fire departments? One wonders. But as B says: "I have no ambition. I am not base enough to hold a conviction."

Giles, sweet Giles, ever the suitor. He persuaded me the antisuffrage papers the women were reading (". . . educated women would stay away from the polls . . . present relations between men and women are all that could be desired . . .") were making me crimson with vexation, and he insisted we escape. We went to the dining room and sipped punch and he put down his cup and kissed me. "I want to embrace your unclothed body," he said, his words squishing at me through the kiss. "I dream of your intimacy. I picture your head on my pillow. I don't care a fig that you're married. Edward is my valued friend and has nothing to do with this. I've loved you since we took dancing class together." He tried to kiss me again but I twisted his ear. He yowled like a cat, yanked his head away and I left him by the punch bowl, sweet fool. Did Father treat Madame Baldwin this way? Probably so.

I have no desire for Giles, but the idea of a lover is taking hold. It has everything to do with resisting my age, for I will be thirty soon. I know how vain and foolish this is, but it is no less real for that. Also I must punish Edward for despoiling me. I sought it, yes, but he did it, as he should have, or I would not have married him. But I cannot forgive him. He does not yet understand the craft of dying. I wonder, shall I be truly beautiful all my life?

The second diary: October 17, 1908
Giles arrived this morning in a frenzy but would not say what was causing it. I made him tea to calm him, and it did. He asked for Edward and when I said he was in New York working on the production of his new play he responded, "As I thought. Are you separated?" I told him Edward and I had been moving apart with glacial slowness, and distance was having antithetical effects, a growing sense of peace, through solitude and the absence of an intolerable presence; but also a deepening fury at being abandoned, however justified the abandonment. I told him I loved Edward profoundly, that in his eyes was a melting tenderness I could find in no other man. Without a word Giles took a folded sheet of paper from his coat and handed it to me. At the center was a well-drawn cartoon of a minotaur cavorting on a theater stage with two near-naked women with the heads of cows, while another and smaller minotaur with excessively large horns was watching from the theater's front row. Beneath the cartoon were six lines of verse:

Your little wife's gone to the city again
To dance on the stage with her partners in sin.

So she and the scribe and the actress will play
Their bovinish games in Gomorrah today,
The ladies disporting like September Morns,
While you sit at home cultivating your horns.

Of course the verse concerns Edward and Melissa Spencer, common gossip by this time, and I have ignored it. But the involvement of Felicity comes as a shock to Giles and a surprise to me; and I saw his frenzy return as a twitch in his left eye. He found the poem in his mailbox this morning. And during the night someone put a severed bull's head on his porch. I wept for the shame of it, for all our shame. I felt extremely close to Giles at this moment, as if what was happening to us with such sudden force was a form of transcendence, thrusting us naked together into some underworld dungeon for abuse by obscene devils. Giles's face was collapsed and flushed with tears, and I then decided to disrobe for him, rid myself of blouse, skirt, petticoat, knickers, shoes, stockings, all. I stood before him as he once said he wanted me, and his weeping ceased. I sat and let him study me, giving him not my body, but the part of my soul that lives in shadow. I told him not to touch me; nor had he betrayed any such plan. He stared at me and we didn't speak, but I felt glorious, basking in the light of my dear friend's wan smile. He stood up and took my chin in his right hand and kissed me just once, then said, "You are the vestal goddess of sublime pain." I had banished his frenzy.

EDWARD GOES TO THE SLAUGHTERHOUSE

June 11, 1910

IT WAS ALREADY late afternoon when Edward closed Katrina's diary. He hitched up the horse he called Galway Kate to his demilandau and rode out to the Cudahy slaughterhouse in West Albany. Cattle were being led out of a storage pen and up an inclined wooden runway onto the killing floor of the huge wooden shed, where Edward told a foreman he had urgent business with Clubber. Clubber, the foreman said, worked as a splitter, and Edward found him, heavy cleaver in hand, halving the backbone of a dead cow. Edward called his name, and Clubber turned and stared at Edward, then finished cutting the beast and handed the cleaver to a man beside him to cope with the next carcass. Clubber spoke to the foreman, then limped toward Edward, who was trying not to retch from the stench of the gutted animals. Clubber rinsed blood off his hands with a hose, and dried them on his trousers, which were full of bloodstains.

"Hey, Ed, what got you out here? I ain't ever seen you out here."

"You got a few minutes, Clubber?"

"I can take ten minutes."

They walked out of the shed to Edward's carriage.

"We'll go have a drink."

"Quick one's all," said Clubber.

"Get up here."

They rode to George Karl's saloon and Edward bought the beer. Clubber pinched himself a piece of beef on an onion slice from the lunch counter and sat at a table.

"Putting the bull's head on Giles's porch, what exactly happened? Tell it again, Clubber."

"I told it twenty hundred times."

"Once more."

"Cully Watson says help him with the joke. Kill the bull, cut its head, leave it down at Giles's, hell of a joke, you know it, he'll wake up and say, 'Hey, that's a dead bull on my porch. Son bitch,' he'll say, 'who'd do a thing like that?' "

"What did Cully do on the porch? Anything you remember?"

"Lifted the head with me."

"What else?"

"Said where to set it."

"Did he have a piece of paper?"

"Paper?"

"With some lines of verse on it."

"What verse?"

"Any verse at all. Whatever you remember."

"Verse."

"What about the paper?"

Clubber drank some beer and searched for the paper.

"I guess he coulda had a paper."

"What'd he do with it?"

"I don't know. Put it in the mailbox?"

"That's right. He put it in Giles's mailbox."

"Yeah. That's it. It was part of the joke. Like a valentine, Cully said. He'll get a valentine in the morning. I forgot that."

Edward handed Clubber the verse he'd copied from Katrina's diary. "Here's what that valentine said."

Clubber's eyes moved across and down the page, up and across, down again, up and across again.

"What's this stuff say?"

"It says in a roundabout way that Giles's wife is down in New

York having sex with two people, a man and a woman. The man is meant to be me. The scribe. That's what it means."

"That ain't true."

"You're right. It's all wrong."

"No, that ain't true on the valentine. It was a joke."

"Wasn't a joke, Clubber."

"It was a joke, I'm telling you. Cully said it was a joke. We laughed like hell at the joke. Just a goddamn dead-bull joke, Ed. That's all it was, a dead-bull joke."

"When Giles read it he went to New York and murdered his wife, shot me, then blew his own brains out through the top of his head. Nobody thought that was a joke."

"That couldn'ta been why he done it, not the joke. It ain't possible, Ed. He gotta had somethin' else on his mind."

"It was this, Clubber, it was this."

Clubber suffered Edward's words as a succession of blows, a whipped cur cowering from an affectionate hand. He pulled in his shoulder and cried, making no noise. He tried to remove the evidence of such unmanly behavior by rubbing the water off his face, wiping his fingers on his pants. When he did it again, he spread pink streaks of the damp cow blood on his cheeks and around his eyes.

"Couldn't be. It ain't true."

"Wasn't a joke, Clubber."

"I wouldn'ta hurt Giles or 'specially you. You know that, Ed."

"I know that, Clubber."

Clubber made a noise in his throat, an involuntary blubbering, and ducked his head below table level so none could see. He coughed, a fake cough, and smeared his face in new places with the pink cow blood.

"Who put Cully up to it?"

Clubber only stared.

"Was it Maginn?"

"Maginn?"

After Edward revealed to Clubber the valentine's fatal message, Clubber hid himself in the darkest corner of the attic of his two-

story home on Van Woert Street. His sister Lydie saw his lunch pail
and knew he'd come home but could not find him. When Clubber
heard her step on the attic stairs he climbed out the window and
leaped off the roof to kill himself. He broke an arm and an ankle,
and sprained a shoulder, all of which were put in casts or wrapped
by Doc Keegan at St. Peter's Hospital. Lydie took her brother
home from the hospital and when she went to sleep he crawled
back up to the attic and threw himself off the same roof, breaking
a leg and a hip, and earning his ticket to the asylum at Pough-
keepsie.

KATRINA IN THE DRAWING ROOM MIRROR

May 7, 1912

SHE STOOD BEFORE the gilt-framed mirror in the drawing room of
her home, primping, reimposing a straying hair, ordering the lines
of her solid-gray, V-necked satin dress, its skirt gathered into soft
billows at the front to reveal stockinged ankles, the shocking fash-
ion at Auteuil this year. She studied what remained of the forty-
seventh year of her beauty. It was persistent, vegetative, clarion.
In her own reversed eyes it seemed less fragile now than when
she married him and had worried about her too-emphatic cheek-
bones, the early lines at the corners of her eyes. Such empty
concern. What does all that mean to anyone now? To him? To
other men?

The men in the mirror, behind her. At her. Always at her, in
memory or dream, or with their need, or their plangent sorrow at
the leave-taking, or their eyes that improve with reversal. And their
alcoholic breath on your neck.

She has known the joy of beauty. But, he wrote, joy is one of her
most vulgar adornments, while melancholy may be called her illus-
trious spouse, a strain of beauty that has nothing to do with sorrow.

She had begun the day knowing her obligations and desires, an
unusual rising, life rarely so orderly for Katrina. She remembered

seeing her father, and dreaming of a monkey, knew what Mrs. Squires should make for breakfast: turkey hash, her mother's favorite, and pumpkin patties, knew the tasks of this consequential morning, knew that revelation would greet her afternoon.

She had bathed, dressed, and, first order, taken down her large black leather shoulder bag and opened it on the bed. From her clothes hamper, where she had put it for safekeeping last night, she took her mother's jewel case and put it in the bottom of the bag. She walked to the third-floor storeroom and unlocked the steamer trunk her father had bought for her trip to London and presentation at court. She rummaged under that famous dress of white chiffon over white silk in which she had made her deep curtsy before Queen Victoria, and she lifted out the seven identical leather-bound diaries of her life. She dropped the key inside the trunk, closed it.

In her room she put six of the dairies in her bag. The remaining one (1896–98) she opened to the page where lay a newspaper clipping of a baseball player photographed in close-up as he throws a ball. Francis of the excellent face.

She raised her glance to the window and looked out at the maple tree in the garden where she'd seen him perched on a branch, sawing another branch above his head. Her valentine in the tree. And she had immediately, then, dressed herself naked, in sun hat and evening slippers, and walked out onto the back piazza to induct the young man into her life. And didn't they love each other so well after that induction? Oh they did.

She built shrines to their love: in her bureau, on her dressing table, on the shelf above the bathtub: a piece of paper on which he'd written both their names: Francis Aloysius Phelan and Katrina Selene Taylor, a snippet of the green canvas he'd wrapped around her when he carried her naked in from the piazza, coins he'd held in his hand, a rag of a shirt he'd left with her, a book with the poems she'd read to him, a handkerchief stained with their love. The shrines were palpable proof of time memorious, when love lived in the next house and came to call.

Until one day it did not. And she destroyed the shrines.

She looked at the clipping, his face scowling at the unseen baserunner he is about to throw out at first, scowling at the hidden Katrina he is about to throw out of his life.

She read the open page of the diary:

The end of summer, 1898:
If you saw me plunge a knife into myself would it baffle you? Would you think it a miracle? Do you understand what I mean when I say I have no ability to slide in and out of love? Would you be tempted to pull the knife out of me and cut off my face? Would you kiss me while I bled through my eyes?

She considered ripping the clipping in half, but did not. She put it between pages of the diary, put the diary into the bag, and went downstairs to breakfast.

"I dreamed of pumpkin last night," she said to Mrs. Squires, who was serving her breakfast. "Does that mean anything?"

"Did you eat the pumpkin?" Mrs. Squires asked.

"No, it was just pulp and I threw it at a monkey."

"Monkeys could mean sharpers are after you, so watch out, Mrs. D. But pumpkin is nice. Pumpkin means happiness. Unless you eat it, and then I'm afraid it means trouble's coming."

"The monkey was a collapsed doll, sitting on a high perch, and I hated it. I hit it with a handful of pumpkin and it came to life."

"So the monkey ate the pumpkin. You'd best be careful today, Mrs. D."

"I shall indeed, Mrs. Squires."

She relished her food, the taste of bygone breakfasts, when her mother shopped and arranged the daily menu. As she swallowed a forkful of the creamy turkey hash the telephone rang in the hall-way. She heard Loretta answer, heard her footsteps coming toward the dining room.

"Martin is on the wire from New York, Missus Daugherty," Loretta said, and Katrina went quickly to the telephone.

"Martin?" she said into the mouthpiece. "This is your mother who loves you. Where are you?"

"A hotel lobby on Fourteenth Street."

"Are you coming home?"

"I'm thinking about it."

"You should stop thinking about it and get on the train. Your father's play opens in four days."

"I know that, Mother."

"Are you coming to see it?"

"That's what I'm thinking about."

"Martin, my sweet and only child, please stop thinking and make your decision. You no longer hate your father. You told me so yourself."

"That's right. I don't hate him."

"Then come and be with him for his play. It will be a momentous event."

"For some people."

"For more than you suppose. Now you must come, Martin. You can't hide from the reality of your life. You must confront it and see what it looks like. Your mother insists. Do you hear what she's saying?"

"I believe I'll be coming."

"You surely will?"

"I believe I will."

"How very, very good that is. Oh how very, very good, Martin. I was afraid you'd fail me. Is there anything else you want to tell me?"

"I'm staying at Father's apartment in the Village. I've just taken over the rental, as he suggested."

"You're such a sensible young man. I'm so proud of you, Martin, so proud. Have we finished with our talk?"

"I told you I would call."

"And so you have. And I told you I would do all in my power to make the rest of your life as harmonious as possible with your father. I do mean that, Martin. I verily do."

"I believe you do, Mother. I'll see you tomorrow."

"You've made me very happy, Martin."

"I'm glad for that, Mother."

"Then goodbye, my sweet boy. Goodbye."

And she placed the receiver on its hook.

She went back to the table, her mind sprinting into the day ahead of her. She sat down to finish her breakfast, but she could not. She took one forkful of hash for old times' sake, then went to the drawing room, where she had left her bag and her hat.

She stood before the mirror, primping, reimposing a straying hair. Her eye swept the reflected room behind her, the room she had created in her own image, and she saw herself unbuttoning Francis's shirt, saw his hand cautiously moving down her shoulder to touch her naked breast for the first time, to touch her scar. Do you like my scar, Francis?

She shook the image away, took her new hat with the ostrich plumes off the table and put it on, pale-gray, wide-brimmed hat that matches her shocking dress. She centered the hat on her head, pinned it to the crown of her hair, which was still the color of the gilded mirror. Maginn, behind her, raised a hand to touch that hair he so worshiped.

"You didn't deserve to have this happen," he said.

He touched the shoulder of her dress, moved his face so close that she smelled the liquor on his breath.

"I saw it coming. Why would he do this to you?"

He touched her bare neck. In the mirror she saw the faces of persistent desire, and behind them the will to persistent desire.

"It should be enough for any man to make love to a woman like you. Having you in my arms is worth any amount of mayhem and murder."

She let him turn her around, and as she did she saw the portraits of her parents staring at her. Why do you allow this slumcrawler to touch you, Katrina? Why do you even allow him in the house? Maginn gripped her arms and kissed her. When she could again see his face he was smiling.

"Shall we sit down?"

They sat on the sofa facing the fireplace and he held her hand in his.

"The anger must be consuming you."

He put one hand on her thigh.

"I was in New York when it happened. I talked to a chambermaid who went in to clean his rooms one day and they didn't hear her key. They were all in bed, making peculiar love. And Felicity was there. The maid knew her."

He moved his hand between her thighs, spreading them, and with one finger began slowly pulling up her skirt.

"There are ways to reciprocate," he said.

She turned away from the mirror and crossed the room to the fireplace. She picked up the black iron poker and walked back to the mirror and smashed it with the poker. Mrs. Squires came running from the dining room.

"Are you all right, Mrs. D?"

"Perfectly fine, Mrs. Squires. I broke the mirror. Will you tell Loretta to sweep up the glass and throw the mirror in the trash. Then move my father's portrait into its place."

"I'll tell her right away."

"I have to go to the bank and the theater. I'll be back this afternoon."

"Very good, Mrs. D."

"The turkey hash was excellent, Mrs. Squires."

"Like your mother made, was it?"

"Exactly like Mother made."

Katrina looped the strap of her bag over her shoulder and left the house, her ostrich plumes bobbing as she walked.

KATRINA SITS FOR HER
PORTRAIT, WITH A FLOWER

IN THE MACDONALD photographic studio on Broadway and
Maiden Lane, the studio favored by eminent Albanians, Katrina
confirmed with the secretary her appointment for a portrait sitting.
She sat down to wait and the secretary stared at her exposed ankles, one stockinged leg visible up to the shinbone.

"Is something wrong?" Katrina asked the secretary. "You seem
to be staring at my dress."

"Oh, nothing wrong at all, Madam. It's a lovely dress. I've just
never seen one like it."

"Do you like it?"

"I wouldn't have the courage to wear it."

"That's a very silly thing to say. One may wear whatever one
chooses to wear."

"Yes, Ma'am."

Pirie MacDonald, the photographer who had established the
studio, came out of an inner office in his tailcoat and greeted
Katrina who shook his hand without standing up.

"Your secretary finds my dress unusual," she said.

"Does she?" MacDonald stared at her legs, nodded. "Shall we
go into the studio?"

He entered behind her and motioned her to a seat in front of a pastoral backdrop with a sky full of clouds. She shook her head.

"That will not do," she said. "I do not want to be photographed with clouds."

"Whatever you say, Madam."

He moved the backdrop to one side, revealing a black backdrop behind it.

"Nor do I want blackness," Katrina said.

"White, then?" And he moved the black backdrop aside, revealing the white wall.

"Do you have any yellow?"

"Color doesn't show in the photograph, Madam."

"But color is there, whether it shows or not."

"It's white or that's it, I'm afraid."

"Then let it be white."

She sat in the chair he placed in front of the empty whiteness while he organized the placement of lights, creating the fall of shadow on her face. "When will the photo be ready?"

"Beginning of the week."

"You'll deliver, of course."

"Of course." He was under his focusing cloth, adjusting the camera lens. "You'll want a torso portrait, I assume. From the waist up?"

"Not at all. I want the entire body."

She moved her legs to give greatest visibility to her ankles. MacDonald came out from under his cloth.

"Is this how you want to be seen in the photo?" he asked, indicating her ankles.

"It's for my husband."

"Very lucky man, your husband."

"No, he's not a lucky man. His life is a disaster, and much of it is my doing."

"I'm sure you're too cruel to yourself, Madam."

"I'm not cruel at all. This is just how it happened to be. One is what one is, one does what one does. Isn't that how you find it?"

"I'm not much on philosophy, Madam."

"But in taking pictures you must see in people's faces how they are."

"Sometimes I think I do, but other times I know what I see is only an illusion. From what I see here, I'm sure this photo will cheer up your husband."

"I hope you are right."

"Then relax, Madam," he said as he hid himself beneath the cloth, "relax."

"I have no intention of relaxing," Katrina said. "You'll have to photograph me as I am."

"Don't move. And look into the camera."

"Wait!" she said, for she suddenly remembered Femmitie Staats, defined forever in her painting by her flirtatious smile; and Katrina wondered which feature of hers people would fix upon as definitive. She loathed the idea of its being her avant-garde ankles. Then she saw the dried sunflower in a vase on a corner table in the studio, and she spoke up, told the photographer she wished to redesign herself, and would he leave her for a few moments?

The billowy V-neck of her dress was adjustable by hidden buttons, two of which she undid, allowing the neck to open to the edges of her shoulders. The separation of her breasts then became visible, but she concealed most of that with the sunflower, whose stem she snapped to shorten it, then tucked the stem inside her bodice. In her mirror image she had become different, new yet again. And, for the first time, the top of her white, oval scar from the Delavan was visible to the world, above the edge of her dress.

Could one call this appearance brazen?

She thought not. Some might suggest that a flaw such as a scar should be hidden forever, but she disagreed.

She called to the photographer to return, and he raised an eyebrow at what he saw, then proceeded to take what would be unarguably the most important photograph of his later life. In it Katrina's hair is symmetrically divided in an inverted V that falls with slight convex curves from the center of her forehead to the edges of her eyebrows, not one hair straying. Her sharply patrician nose is half in soft shadow, her mouth a small smile that says "I understand," and there are deep oval shadowings that enhance her eyes, render them patient with the melancholy she so covets. She is looking directly at us and into us, her torso slightly rightward, her yellow sunflower an oblique presence, her left shoulder in a gently aggressive forward thrust, for she is yielding, but with a will that only very reluctantly recognizes the inevitable; yet it does recognize it. Her ankles, a statement of rebellion, do not dominate the photograph as MacDonald thought they might; but they color it, as Katrina's radical exploration of love colored her entire life, and the lives of those around her.

With the making of this picture MacDonald would elevate himself, for a time, to the status of master photographer of eastern American beauty. Women of privilege, having once seen this photo, would come to Albany from as far as Boston and Manhattan to be photographed by him. But no other photo he took in these years would approach in vividness the image of Katrina and her sunflower with the pale yellow petals: two kindred blossoms of nature's intelligence, caught at the peak of their elegant desiccation.

KATRINA DEPOSITS SOME
VALUABLES IN THE
BANK VAULT

KATRINA WALKED FROM Broadway up State Street to the State National Bank, where her grandfather Lyman and her father had been directors in their time; the oldest bank in the city, where Archie Van Slyke was an assistant vice president, still. She saw Archie at his desk in a far corner of the main banking room, in his tight suit and his pince-nez. He stood to greet her as she walked toward him, and from the lethargic way he moved she decided he was still drinking too much.

With the Van Slyke and Taylor fortunes behind him, Archie had entered Albany's banking world with flourish and promise. But he skidded at the death of Adelaide, and moped forward in life, focused on the bottle, never remarrying, keeping himself humbled and blurred. Yet he held his job, kept his modest title, one reason being that Geraldine had always placed unqualified trust in his handling of her once-substantial accounts.

Katrina always thought of Archie when she remembered what Henry James had told Edward and her during their luncheon in New York in 1903. When he thought of Albany, Henry said, he remembered his father's stories about his own contempo-

raries, all of them men with great promise and romantic charm, all
of them, in his father's eyes, eventually ending badly, as badly as
possible.

"Oh dear, Archie," she said as she sat beside his desk, "this is a
sad errand. I closed Mother's house last night."

"How is she?"

"Depressed. But the good of it is she no longer has to fear fore-
closure. She'll do fine in the apartment. And she's still in the old
neighborhood."

"I knew it was happening," Archie said. "Such a pity. Such a
magnificent house it was."

"I've taken a few pieces of special memory, but the rest is off to
be auctioned. I bring valuables for our box in your vault. Mother
had a safe for them at home, but I do not."

As he prepared the paper for her to sign, Katrina saw the de-
scending panorama of Archie's entire life, culminating in the
whiskey-blotch of his face; and she realized precisely how this, too,
had happened. She would have to tell him.

"We'll go in now," Archie said, and together they walked across
the bank to the armed guard, and Archie presented him with
Katrina's identification card; and they entered. Katrina left her bag
on the table in the coupon room, and walked into the great vault of
the bank with Archie. Together they opened the combination lock
on the Daugherty safe deposit box, and Katrina carried the box
back to the table.

"I'll be a few minutes with this," she said.

"Ring the wall buzzer and I'll come back," Archie said.

She took the jewel case out of her bag and placed all that was
in it on the table: her mother's diamond tiara, the silver cream
pitcher from the Cromwell tea service, a pair of gold cuff links in-
scribed with her father's initials in Old English script, two gold
rings she and Adelaide had outgrown in childhood, the single
strand of pearls Lyman had given Geraldine on her sixteenth
birthday, and a miscellany of gold and silver bracelets that might
not be gold and silver, since Geraldine had yielded most jewelry of
value to rescue her husband from debt. This was what remained
of the Taylor fortune, excepting what would come from the auc-

tion and the sale of the house, some of which would clear her mother's debt to tradesmen, doctors, and lawyers, the rest to go into the trust fund that would pay for Geraldine's modest room and board for the rest of her life. The melancholy management of reduced expectations.

Katrina took two silk scarves from her bag, wrapped the tiara, pitcher, and cuff links (a set of rainy-day surprises for Edward) in one, the rest of the items in the other. She saw that, as now packed, the deposit box would not accept all she wanted to put into it. She took out the family documents, their birth certificates, and the endowment agreement under which Lyman gave an annuity to Edward, the deeds to the Colonie Street house and the Daugherty house on Main Street, and two plays by Edward she had copied and put here for safekeeping without his knowing: *Pyramus and Thisbe*, which had since been published and no longer needed to be here, and *Lunar Majesty*, his play about a woman's courtship, marriage, and early estrangement from her husband. Katrina cherished this play for its compassion and insight—into her, of course—she the enduring heroine of all of Edward's works. She opened the manuscript to a page and read:

> THE HUSBAND: I'm convinced she's walled in behind the energy of her derangement, sane as anyone alive, mad as the queen of Bedlam—the stigmata, the sickness, the lesions visible in her eyes and the clutch of her hand. Such a marvel of womanhood, as pure and as fated as Eve before the serpent.

"A bit overstated, Edward," Katrina said aloud.

Then she closed the manuscript, laid it flat in the deposit box, arranged the diaries atop it, then put in the jewels wrapped in their scarves. She folded *Pyramus and Thisbe* into her leather bag, closed the box, and rang the buzzer for Archie. He was waiting outside the door. Together they reentered the vault, secured the box in its place, and left the vault.

"I saw my father last night at the house," Katrina said as they went out.

Archie stopped, looked at her, took off his pince-nez.

"I was standing in his office," she said, "and I realized he was in the cellar. I went down with a candle and found him sitting on a stool by the pipe where the city water comes in. The pipe was dripping water onto his shoulder. He was wearing his small spectacles and an old overcoat, which was quite wet. He was hunched over and looked very pitiful. We stared at each other until I summoned the courage to say, 'I would take you upstairs, Father, but there's nothing up there now.' He continued to stare at me, and the water dripped onto his unruly hair."

Archie looked away from Katrina, spoke to the floor.

"You know, Katrina, of course you know, that your father is dead. You were at his burial."

"Of course I was, of course I know that."

"I suppose these things can happen."

"Father blamed Edward for Adelaide's death, but I was the one. Edward was only doing what he knew I wanted."

"You can't blame yourself for such things, Katrina. You seem a bit skewed today, frankly. You should see a doctor."

"I'm very clear on it, Archie. I truly am."

Her voice was as bright as morning.

"If I hadn't been what I was, Edward and I wouldn't have needed to make peace with the family. If we all hadn't gone to that dinner of reconciliation, Adelaide and my father wouldn't have died, and you wouldn't have ruined your career with drink."

"I have hardly done that, Katrina. You are ill."

"It's you who are ill, Archie, and I'm sorry I had a hand in it."

"You'll soon be taking blame for the weather."

"Perhaps I shall. It's quite uncanny what one sets in motion by being oneself."

She stood up and extended her hand.

"Thank you so much, Archie. I must go up to the Hall now and see a bit of the dress rehearsal of Edward's play."

"Yes, I saw a notice in the paper."

"I believe he's written the tragedy of our lives. And do stop drinking, Archie. You're such a good man without it."

"You should learn to mind your own business, Katrina."

"Yes, I suppose I should. But I have so very little business to mind."

KATRINA WATCHES
THE FLAMING CORSAGE

She sits alone at the rear of the orchestra
In Harmanus Bleecker Hall,
Albany's premier
Theater

She sees only Act Four, Scene One

The text of the scene:

The City Club Tea Room on Elk Street (ladies only),
summer, 1910. One round white wicker table, two
matching chairs, one potted palm tree in white pot.

MARINA and CLARISSA are seated at table with white
lamp with white shade, a pot of tea, two cups and
saucers, spoons, two small plates, and, in the center of
the table, a plate of small sandwiches made from white
bread with crusts removed.

Both women are elegantly dressed in long, white dresses
with colossal hats. MARINA's hat is a garden of puffy

white ostrich plumes. CLARISSA's hat is a circular fountain of long, narrow white feathers.

MARINA: Will you have tea?

CLARISSA: If you please.
             (Marina pours tea into both cups.)
             You must wonder about my letter.

MARINA: Not at all.

CLARISSA: I thought it important to write you.

MARINA: Did you? Why was that?

CLARISSA: I thought we should discuss Miles.

MARINA: *Did* you? Why was *that*?

CLARISSA: He was so odd.

MARINA: You're absolutely right. Shooting his wife that way. Then shooting himself. Odd.
             (Marina sips her tea, holds cup in air.)
             Miles suffered from an excess of fastidiousness.
             (She sips tea again, puts cup down.)
             He was appalled by its absence in others.

CLARISSA: Miles was quite wrong about one thing. He thought his wife and your husband were paramours.

MARINA: But it was *you* and my husband who were paramours.

CLARISSA: We were the best of friends.

MARINA: And now that's all past. Now Miles is dead and my husband considers you a well-poisoner.

CLARISSA: I understand your anger.

MARINA: My anger faded long ago, replaced by other emotions.

CLARISSA: I won't ask what they are.

MARINA: I'm not sure I could say what they are. They're quite mysterious.

CLARISSA: Your husband thinks me a well-poisoner?

MARINA: He blames himself, but thinks you spawned the disaster.

CLARISSA: How does he think I did that?

MARINA: Through Mangan, who conceived the plot to expose your love nest, the most successful creative act of his life.
(She sips her tea.)

CLARISSA: Mangan never forgave Miles for the fireman's-wife joke.

MARINA: Nonsense.

CLARISSA: He was so humiliated.

MARINA: Mangan is unhumiliatible.

CLARISSA: Mangan is really quite sensitive.

MARINA: Mangan lacks fastidiousness.
(Pause.)
He told me you were his constant paramour, even when you were seeing my husband. Dreadful to reveal such things.

CLARISSA: Did Mangan say that?
(She sips her tea.)
He's such a liar.

MARINA: He did not seem to be lying.
(She proffers plate of sandwiches.)
Sandwich?

CLARISSA: Thank you.
(Clarissa takes sandwich, bites it.)
Delicious.
(Marina takes sandwich from plate and smells it.)

MARINA: Raw fish. How repellent.
(She puts sandwich on her own plate, wipes her fingers with napkin.)

Mangan has always envied my husband. They were like brothers once, but he envied my husband's social position, envied his marrying me, envied his success in the theater, envied his self-possession.
(Pause.)
My husband was the true target in the love-nest conspiracy, not poor, simple Miles.
(She lifts teapot.)
Tea?

CLARISSA: If you please.
(Marina pours tea.)
Mangan told me he once had Miles's wife. In a Pullman compartment on the train from Albany to New York.

MARINA: I did say Mangan lacked fastidiousness, did I not?

CLARISSA: But he does seem to know things.
(Pause.)
He told me you took a seventeen-year-old neighbor boy as the light of your life.
(She sips her tea.)
He believes there is no such thing as fidelity. "The fidelity fallacy," he calls it.

MARINA: He stole that phrase from a speech in my husband's unfinished play. Do you know the rest of that speech? "No one understands the disease of infidelity until it's upon you. And then you are transfigured. Of course you have your reasons for what you do, but they are generally misleading."
(She sips her tea.)
Quite an accurate speech, wouldn't you say?

CLARISSA: I'm sure you know better than I. Mangan also told me he had *you,* two days after the shooting.

MARINA: He tried often with me, but never succeeded. I'm not as diverse as you in these matters.

CLARISSA: You have such lofty airs.

MARINA: And you are from womanhood's lowest register. You linked yourself to my husband when he was a rising star, and now, after you've risen on his back, you want to destroy what remains of his life as a fallen star.

CLARISSA: I loved him truly.

MARINA: You began as a frivolous soubrette, full of intrigue, and in short order you've risen to become a sublime slut. Do your sluttish things, as you must, but don't speak to me of love.
(Marina picks up teapot.)
Love is vertical. You are relentlessly horizontal.
(She proffers teapot.)
More tea?

KATRINA RUMINATES ON
WHAT SHE HAS SEEN

HE MAKES ME cleverer than I am. He knows things I do not know about Maginn. I don't know how he knew Maginn came to see me, and I doubt very much Maginn had Felicity in a Pullman. She wouldn't. Would she? Edward believes he knows the truth about my life without him. "I know of your dalliances," he once said. "Of course you don't," I told him. He will come to know some of what was. His writing is acute, and bright people will admire it, but the clergy will try to have the play closed. No one can say such things publicly. Edward knows this. He is flaunting his play. "You made me the villainous eater of broken meats," he is saying. "Here then, see what raw fish such a man offers you."

He is obviously finished with that woman. I do like the well-poisoner line. I wish I had said it. He is giving a shape to the chaos that overtook us. What he said at dinner — when the matter is ready the form will come. I wonder did he see me sitting in the theater? He did not come down. Perhaps he thought I would go backstage. No. He would assume I would not wish to confront them all. He must not have seen me. Nonsense, if he thought I could not face up to people. I've recovered. I've recovered from everything. It's depressing how total my recovery is; as if the condition had not been serious. No one can know what the wound was like. No one would care to know. Even Edward could see only the blood, the scab, the scar. There will be a photograph of my recovery. It's depressing how easily we reconcile the unthinkable. I must let Edward know why I never told him about Giles, and Maginn's doggerel. How to tell him? I want no argument. Tell him also what no one ever knew about Felicity. But I saw it. Tell Edward these things now. Yes. Answer all questions. What was I supposed to do with my life? Was it correct, what I did? Was it worth doing? Write him a letter. A letter, of course. When the matter is ready the form will come.

She left the theater and walked to the cabstand in front of the Armory, full of the memory of significant life on the Hall's grand stage. There she had seen Caruso and Pavlova and met John McCormack after he'd thrilled her with that old ballad *("Oh! hast thou forgotten how soon we must sever? Oh! hast thou forgotten this day we must part?")*. She had watched Duse and Maude Adams and Richard Mansfield and countless others play out their charades of life, she had danced with Edward on the false floor that covered the theater seats for Governor Roosevelt's inaugural ball. And this week Edward's people, you among them, Katrina, will come to life on that enormous stage. And everyone's legend will grow.

Katrina's hat was so large that she had to tip her head sideways in order to step into the cab.

She entered her empty house, the servants gone until dinner, and left her bag and her hat in the drawing room. She made tea for herself in the kitchen and carried it on a tray to Edward's office, where she set it atop his desk. She sat in Edward's chair and took one of his lined tablets from the drawer. She sipped the tea as she considered the questions she would write answers to on the tablet.

"What, really, was my destiny?" she wrote.

She put her head down on the desk in acquiescence to the drowsiness the question evoked in her. She slept for she knew not how long, and awoke smelling smoke. She went to the window of the office and parted the curtains to see the Christian Brothers school next door in flames. It was clear to her that the fire would make the leap to this room in a matter of minutes. She went back to Edward's chair and put her head down on his desk. The smoke was familiar in her mouth. She had breathed fire before.

EDWARD AND KATRINA
REVISIT THE CEMETERY

May 10, 1912

AFTER THE HOUSE burned, and Katrina died in his arms, Edward moved what was left of his life into a parlor suite at the Kenmore Hotel and began the process of gently evicting the Cohallon family from Emmett and Hanorah's Main Street house: his house now, his only house now. He put Katrina in the hands of Ebel Campion, whose undertaking parlors were only two blocks from where she died, with instructions that there would be no wake, only a funeral mass in Sacred Heart church, and then private burial. He would not abide strangers ogling her corpse.

The buzzards were already at work on the leftover carrion from the Love Nest scandal, writing how the debauchery of the ogre Daugherty had shamed Katrina, hastened her death; and cheering—were they not?—for the innocent Melissa, who had replied to the evil done her by gaining much-deserved movie stardom. There they perched, at the edge of Edward's life, anticipating new morsels from *The Flaming Corsage*, which would open May 11, the fourth day after Katrina's death; for the show must go on *now*, Mr. Ogre, or not at all.

Sacred Heart church was filled, even to standing room, and hundreds more jammed the church steps, and Walter Street's sidewalk, twenty minutes before the small cortege arrived. Six bearers carried Katrina's coffin up the steps into the church, photographers recording her ascent, then moving their tripods to focus on Edward, impeccably tailored in black suit with cutaway coat and beaver hat, stepping down from the first carriage, with Martin next, dressed like his father, and then the heavily veiled Geraldine, triadic study in family distance. Geraldine's brother, Ariel, and Archie Van Slyke came in the second carriage, then other relatives, friends.

As they entered the church in procession, Edward saw, first, the blaze of color on the altar: the dozen baskets of yellow flowers he had sent to brighten the solemnity for Katrina, then saw, with sharper focus, faces from North Albany, Colonie Street, Elk Street: Francis and Annie Phelan, and old Iron Joe with them; and Jack and Ruthie McCall, she refusing to measure his eye; and the Phelans: Peter, Chick, Molly, and Tommy, all in one pew; and Bishop Sloane, flanked by a brace of Minor Canons, bowing ecclesiastically to Geraldine as she passed him; and so many, many more neighbors and forever-nameless witnesses to the lamentable truth: that Katrina Selene Taylor Daugherty is no more.

Father Loonan, without the stamina to say mass, sat in trembling witness on the altar, as Edward had asked of him: Katrina's counselor in the faith when she converted. Three other priests would celebrate Katrina's passing with a solemn high mass, and Father Loonan, at the proper moment, feeble but clear of speech, and wearing his simple cassock and surplice, would stand and read the Gospel, not only from the mass for the dead, but also from the mass for the previous day on the liturgical calendar, as if the two Gospels were one; and Edward found the addition of the latter Gospel more than accidental redundancy: ". . . You are the salt of the earth; but if the salt lose its savor, wherewith shall it be salted? It is good for nothing any more, but to be cast out, and to be trodden on by men. You are the light of the world. A city seated on a mountain cannot be hid. Neither do men light a candle and put it under a bushel, but upon a candle-stick, that it may shine to all that are in the house . . ."

Yea, verily, Father. Edward will make Katrina shine for all in the house. Come and see his play.

❊ ❊ ❊

Ebel Campion and his bearers carried Katrina's coffin out of the church to the hearse, then drove it not to St. Agnes Cemetery, as expected, but back to the funeral home, where it remained for hours, until the last of the snuffling press had abandoned its watch. The undertaker then put the coffin into the closed wagon he used for picking up corpses, a vehicle never pressed into cemetery service before; then, with one bearer who could be trusted to keep his mouth shut, rode to the Kenmore to pick up Edward and Martin, and transported the Daugherty family to Albany Rural Cemetery, to the plot Edward had bought for Katrina, twenty yards from the grove of blue spruces where she had offered up her virginity to him.

Without prayer, the four men lowered her into the newest grave in this gateway to the Protestant beyond, the heaven where Katrina would be most at ease, and watched silently as two gravediggers arrived to bury the coffin and fill the grave with fresh earth. When the workers departed, Edward asked his son, "Do you want to say anything?"

Martin shook his head. "You really need a ritual at this point?"

Edward smiled at the new clarity in Martin, done with adolescence at last, his face refined to a mature handsomeness, a young man who speaks with a quiet fluency that belies the anger Edward sees in him.

"You're a man who uses words, as am I," Edward said.

"I've already spoken my words to her," Martin said.

"Before or after she died?"

"Before."

"That smacks of excellence," Edward said. "I applaud your initiative."

"Your applause sounds like parental pride for what you've instilled in me."

"I think your mother would not want us to argue at her grave."

"She wanted us reconciled."

"And so we are," Edward said. "We're together. We have each other. We have no one else."

"I don't feel reconciled," Martin said. "I seem unable to forgive what you did to us."

"Understandably so. But it's a pity you see the world from only one perspective."

"You mean I should take her madness into consideration? I've watched it since I was a child."

"She wasn't mad, she was original."

Edward took a step forward and spoke to the grave.

"I don't know what she believed," he said, "but it was a belief like none other. She began with God and moved on to death, and made them part of her being. But she abandoned both to astonish her soul. She sought something no one expects out of this life, and sought it with a firm purpose that she defined and executed without the advice or consent of others. She might have been judged an ascetic in another time, for she was much in love with suffering, her own and others'. She was also seraph and voluptuary, of such uncommon ways she seemed to preexist the fall; and there is no name for such a hybrid in our limited world, or our limited heavens. But she does not need justification. Katrina dwelled among us, and we are thankful for that. We will regret forever that she has willfully left us."

"Willfully?" said Martin. "What do you mean?"

"Her time had ended. She knew it."

"The fire killed her."

"Of course it did," said Edward. "It was her element."

EDWARD COMPLETES HIS PLAY AT THE KENMORE HOTEL

IN THE SPRING months when he was trying to finish *The Flaming Corsage*, Edward was accumulating evidence that he owned only half a brain, half a heart, that his talent had decayed, all fire gone from his imagination. With his early plays he had run blindfolded into the unknown and come away with the prize, or believed he had. But now he knew that despite his relentless work, something was missing. This play did not end, it aborted. Three years of writing and he had produced a ridiculous lie, an evasion, a travesty of the truth. Nothing will save it from savagery by all who see it.

There is blood in your mouth, Edward.

The enemy applauds your fate.

He decided Maginn must have lived all his life in this condition: full of desire and effort, but a creative cripple: inadequate strength to imagine the substance of the work, and an intelligence too arrogant to shape it. The love song of the wrong word.

Then Katrina died, and Edward sat at the desk in the parlor of his hotel suite and began a new ending for the play—already in production with the flawed ending. He wrote the night she died; wrote most of the following two days, except for some time with Martin, and arranging the funeral. After the mass, while waiting for the undertaker, he began yet another version of the final scene, one with promise. After the burial he reread the scene and let it stand.

The two as measured distance. The absence that grows in the fertile earth.

He hired the young woman typewriter-copyist in the hotel's office to make three copies, and was at the theater to hand them to the director and actors when they arrived in the evening for the final run-through.

Too late to change this much dialogue, the director said. It absolutely *must* be changed, Edward said. I'll never memorize it in time, the lead actor said. Oh yes, you will, said Edward. And the play opened Saturday night with the final dialogue dictated by Katrina.

Edward watched the performance from the aisle of the parquet. When the houselights went up on the clamor that greeted the end of the play, Edward saw Maginn in a forward box with a woman, and moved toward him immediately. But he was met by the exiting throng and lost Maginn in the crowd.

The play closed after one performance.

"SCANDALOUS PLAY CLOSES"

Albany Argus, *May 13, 1912*

THE FORCES OF decency in the city dealt a sledgehammer death blow to the new play by Edward Daugherty
Saturday night. The opening performance at Harmanus
Bleecker Hall was greeted with hisses at the first scene
of Act Four, and shouts of "unclean" and "filth" were
heard as the play progressed to its conclusion. A score of
people left the theater, which was packed to capacity for
the performance, more than 2,500 seats filled. When the
curtain came down, the hisses and boos were loud and
relentless, especially from the gallery, and extra police
were summoned to move the audience out of the theater.

Yesterday morning Episcopal Bishop Sloane and Catholic Bishop Burke, in concert with Mayor McEwan and
many leading citizens of the city, pressed the owners of
the Hall and the play's producers to cease further performance. At midafternoon the producer announced the
cancellation of the play's two-week run. The Hall's man-
ager said he will offer, in its place, the return of last week's
immensely popular production of *Regeneration*, with Bert

Lytell, the story of an Irish Bowery thug raised to manhood by the power of a woman's prayer.

Daugherty's play, titled *The Flaming Corsage,* purports to be a tragic love story, but is a thinly veiled excursion into the lower regions of human degradation, beginning with the murder, in a "love nest," of an unfaithful wife, who is shot by her husband; and the husband then suicides. It carries on from there through such morally repugnant dialogue as has never been heard on the Albany stage. Some phrases would not be printable in this newspaper under any circumstances, yet they are uttered brazenly by two women characters.

"The shame of Albany" is what Bishop Sloane called the play; Bishop Burke said such a writer should be "damned to hell for such public sin"; and the Mayor, who had not seen the play, said, "From all accounts it is a degenerate assault on American womanhood. And we won't stand for that in this city."

It was agreed yesterday by seasoned theatergoers who saw the play that it is little more than a self-exculpation by the playwright, an apologia for his involvement in the Love Nest Scandal of 1908 in Manhattan, whose events closely parallel those of the play, with names of the characters changed so slightly from their real-life counterparts that all are recognizable. And so the old scandal is rekindled to a bright flame.

LETTER TO THE EDITOR

Albany Argus, *May 14, 1912*

Dear Sir,

I rush to correct the general misapprehension of the play *The Flaming Corsage,* which closed after a single performance on Saturday. The play is seen as a violation of our Magnificent Municipal Moral Code (would that it were!). But it was not that at all, and judgment of it on that basis should be left to the philistines. The play will have, most certainly, a secure place in the history of American theater, as a curiosity. It has kinship with dreadful Ibsen's one great achievement, *Peer Gynt,* and may be as great a literary benchmark as *Beowulf,* that ossified ostrich egg of fictional narrative, though the Daugherty play resembles neither work.

The Flaming Corsage must be judged a failure, a great botch of a work that should probably have been a novel, just as Chekhov's plays, overstuffed with characters and incident, would have shone as novels. Daugherty, the playwright, was, potentially, a novelist of the first rank, but abandoned the genre for playwriting, a major mistake, the success of his last play notwithstanding. That play, *The Masks of Pyramus,* owed its success to its paralleling of *Romeo and Juliet,* just as the Shakespeare work owed its nucleus to Ovid's *Pyramus and Thisbe.* Plagiarism in the arts continues apace.

But *The Flaming Corsage* does have its merits. It casts aside the weeping and wailing of our mouldy melodrama and the contrived realism of our present potpourri of pygmy playwrights, and instead it offers up scenes rich with raw realism, as well as stinging satire of a high order. The bovinish women of the piece, and their hopeless husbands and lovers, all struggle between lofty intentions and hidden animal instincts, much the way Peer Gynt confronts the evil trolls of his life in the Ibsen play.

No one in American theater has ever written with as much insight into the dark quotidian reality as Edward Daugherty. It is a great pity that he is such a paltry buffoon when it comes to organizing his play, and sorting out the fates of his characters. He creates fine china, then destroys it all with his unruly hindquarters.

Like *Beowulf,* which was fated to be unreadable, this play is fated to be judged unplayable by future generations. But it will also be studied as a grotesque curiosity that broke new theatrical ground. It does not surprise me that it was closed, but it was closed for the wrong reasons.

THEATER LOVER
(Name withheld)

EDWARD WRITES A NEW PLAY

July 15, 1912

EDWARD SAT NOW in a long pause, staring out the second-floor window of his workroom at another grotesquely shadowed evening that had become abominably hot. The pages of his nameless play-in-progress lay on the desk beside the marble bust of Persephone, the only artifact of value to survive the fire. And beside that lay Emmett's loaded .32-caliber revolver.

Emmett had bought the pistol to defend himself during labor trouble at the Fitzgibbon foundry, protection against men he'd fought for all his life; for when he became foreman, he became their enemy. Rise in the world and count your friends on your thumb.

"I could shoot it and hit what I shot at," Emmett said, "but I never pulled the trigger in anger, or in fear. It was a useless damn gadget and I knew that the day I bought it."

Edward looked at the pistol. He looked at his pages. He picked up his first page, read the opening scene. Sweat dropped from his forehead onto the paper.

> *Scene One*
> *(The execution chamber of Sing Sing prison. Six* WITNESSES
> *sit on folding chairs facing the empty electric chair.* EXECU-

TIONER *stands near large-handled switch that will activate electric current.*

WARDEN *and* PRIEST *enter with* THOMAS MAGINN, *the prisoner. Two* GUARDS, *escorting* MAGINN, *seat him in electric chair, strap him into it, apply one electrode to calf of his right leg, another to cover his forehead and shaved temples.*

DR. GILES FITZROY *enters, walking ahead of stretcher wheeled in by another* GUARD, *and upon which lies the pale corpse of* EDWARD DAUGHERTY. GILES *motions to* GUARD *where to put stretcher.* GUARD *tips stretcher on its end so that* DAUGHERTY *corpse stands upright, facing the electric chair.)*

GILES (*To* WARDEN):   Is the condemned ready?

WARDEN (*To* PRIEST):   Is he ready, Father?

PRIEST: Frankly, I don't think he has a prayer.

WARDEN: Are you ready, Mr. Maginn?

   (MAGINN *breaks into hysterical laughter, which continues as he speaks.)*

MAGINN: My father collected dead horses for pig food. My mother was a one-armed bitch who took in washing for cowboys. My sister was a whore at age six. My kid brother tortured cats with hatpins. My uncle gouged eyes for a dime. My family was saintly in the extreme.

   (*His laughter subsides somewhat.)*

   I'm a lucky man, the first in my family to be executed for his intelligence. The world will mark today as the day they uselessly martyred a beloved hero, and it will await my resurrection. There's no doubt I'm the

smartest man on the North American continent, given to humility at all hours, ready to
play the fool for any woman with pubic hair.
I also admire them shorn.

(MAGINN's *laughter is gone, his face saddens
gradually. He weeps, then cries openly.*)

The worth of my being is proportionate to
the weight of my written work. The essence
of all power in this life is defiance, malfea-
sance, the pox, the smile, the dollar, and
comprehension of the nature of time, which
is running short. In sum, I'm as unprepared
for death as I was for life. But let's get on
with it.

(MAGINN *is now sobbing, breathing with
difficulty.*)

Red pig blood, orange sunset and evening
star, pale-yellow pig shit, lime-green urine,
blue sky and meadow, indigo clouds, violet
pussy, white horses, whiteness whitening
the white white . . .

(*He stops sobbing, laughs hysterically.*)

WARDEN (*To* GILES):	The condemned is ready.
GILES:	Are you ready, Mr. Daugherty.
DAUGHERTY:	I am.
GILES:	Let it be noted for the record that the eyes of the dead Daugherty have been sewn open to enable him to witness the execution of his murderer, the fugitive whoremonger, the un-requited narcissist. Now, let us proceed.

(*He waves his hand to* EXECUTIONER, *who pulls
switch, sending current into* MAGINN, *who stiff-*

ens. Steam rises from his skull and from his leg. GILES, *checking his pocket watch, waves to* EXECUTIONER, *who turns switch off.* GILES *examines* MAGINN *with stethoscope and holds thermometer against his leg.)*

GILES:

Let it be noted that auscultation indicates the condemned still has a pulse, and the temperature of the skin is one hundred eighty degrees. All skin contacts show notable burn marks. How are you feeling, Mr. Maginn?

MAGINN:

Tip-top.

GILES:

Then let us continue.

(He gestures again to EXECUTIONER, *who pulls switch, with same reaction from* MAGINN. *Not steam but smoke rises from burned flesh.* GILES *times this jolt with his watch, waves to* EXECUTIONER, *who turns off current.* GILES *examines* MAGINN.)*

GILES:

The condemned heart still beats. Temperature at contact points now two hundred fourteen degrees, nicely above boiling point. Crepitation noted throughout. Anterior epithelial cells of the cornea have desquamated from the action of heat. Sclera of left eye bulges at its left corneal junction. Scalp and skin of neck have a dull, purplish hue, with blisters on temples, cheeks, and eyelids. Epidermis at flexure of knee joint has been torn away. How are you feeling, Mr. Maginn?

MAGINN (*Weakly*):

Violet piss, golden pigs.

GILES:

Then let us continue.

(He waves hand again to EXECUTIONER, *etc.)*

Edward stopped reading. He ordered the pages of the play and walked downstairs to the kitchen, the heat no longer tolerable. He pumped water, wet his face, hair, arms. He walked, dripping, to the front porch, sat in his father's rocking chair, and stared at the corner of the porch. The flood this spring had tilted it another fraction of an inch eastward: fittingly askew.

He stared up the empty street and saw his young self walking off it forever (oh yes) and out of this city into worlds no boy, no man on this block, except his father, could even have imagined. Now he was back, solitary Main Streeter: no visitors, curtains drawn, answering no rings of the bell, no knocks, reading no mail, food delivered by Drislane's.

The oaks and the elms are in full leaf, the honeysuckle bush his mother planted in 1859, when the house was new, when Main Street and Edward were new, is a tree now, yielding berries, and the robins are eating them. Nobody hates these leaves, these berries, these robins, the way people hate Edward. Neither will Edward love any of them for their overrated glory, their vaunted beatitude. You think such mindless things deserve love? Love is what you feel during yesterday's lightning storms. And then here come the dogs.

He saw two boys with sticks running down from Broadway, chasing a dog that was leaving them behind, that ran into the horseshoe court between Joe Farrell's and Edward's houses, across Francis Phelan's backyard, and was gone.

"You won't catch him now, boys," Edward said, and the boys stopped and looked at him. "And there's gardens back there. You wouldn't want to run through them."

"He bit me," one boy said.

"Did he draw blood?"

The boy, in short pants, looked at his bare leg. Edward could see a line of blood from calf to ankle.

"Yeah, he got me," the boy said.

"You should go see Doc McArdle," Edward said. "You know where he lives?"

"Doc McArdle is dead," the boy said.

"Is he?"

"His horse kicked him in the head."

The boy bent his leg to look at the wound, spat on it, and rubbed up the trickle of blood with two fingers. He snapped the spit and blood off the fingers, pulled a leaf off an oak tree and wiped the wound.

"I'll put a bandage on it," the second boy said, and he took off the red bandanna he was wearing on his neck and tied it around his friend's wound. The boy who'd been bitten took a few steps, limping.

"It hurts," he said.

He picked up a stone and hurled it at the garden where the dog had fled. The second boy picked up two stones and threw them at the eastern sky that arced toward the bed of the Erie Canal that was: whelps all: the dog, the boys, Edward.

The moon sent down its light to weave an image in the branches of an oak tree, and Edward saw in it Emmett's face: a grid of sinew and wisdom that would not stay in the grave. There, perfectly etched by leaf and moonlight, were the lines of the Emmett nose and jaw, the wry slash of smile, vanishing, then reappearing in the flickering light's gestalt. Keeper of the flame. But there is no longer a flame. Your father is preparing for your departure, Edward.

Under this July moon, now shaped like a battered face, Edward left the porch, walked past the lot where the cattle pens used to be on Champlain Street, parallel to the tracks and the all-but-dead canal. Beyond the canal half a dozen of forty-two sawmills were still active in the Lumber District, which was dying from want of softwood: so many Adirondack pine forests denuded, so few people working in the District that for sixty years gave jobs to men by the swarm: now a zone of quiet. No more overflowing lunch crowds in Black Jack's, no more cardsharps at the tables, no more brawls, no more dead horses in the canal, all work in the foundries now, or over the hill in the West End, at the Central's railroad shops. Purpose vanishing from North Albany, eclipsed like the dead Irish of Connacht. Potential actualized into a living neighborhood. And then? Yes. What, then, is the potential of the *new* actuality?

He walked up Erie Street past the icehouse, and the site of the old wooden Sacred Heart church, where pigs and chickens came to mass, now a vacant lot. He passed the car barns. When he read the *Car Barns* play to his father in his sickbed (for he would not live to see it performed) Emmett had asked:

"Is that fella in the play supposed to be me?"

"Does he sound like you?"

"He does."

"Did you say those things he says?"

"Never."

"So there you are. You and not you, reality and fantasy in one package."

"You're a glib man. If you don't change your ways you'll come to a bad end."

Prophetic.

He turned onto Broadway, bats swooping though the glow of streetlamps, and saw Cappy White with a growler under his arm. Edward hadn't seen Cappy since his son, Bitsy, a softspun boy born without ears, who'd earned candy money eating live frogs for a nickel, went up in flames in church while lighting a candle for his mother, Mamie. Mamie weighed maybe five hundred pounds — nobody ever found a way to weigh her — and grew wider with the years. When Doc McArdle came to examine her dropped stomach she refused him access: "I never showed my front end to anybody but Cappy White. He was the first one, he'll be the last one."

Mamie stayed in the house, could not leave it even for Bitsy's funeral, did not fit into the stairwell. When she died Cappy knocked out siding and two windows, then backed up a derrick to lift her out of bed and carry her to her own funeral. After that he took himself to bed and stayed there, leaving it only to buy food and beer. Hermit of Main Street, punished by the gods for marrying fat and cherishing a freakish child. What peculiar shapes love takes.

"Hi ya, Cappy," Edward said.

"Who's that?"

"Eddie Daugherty."

"Eddie, yeah, you're back. I heard you lost everything."

"That's right, Cappy."

"So did I."

"I know."

"How you livin'?"

"Best way I can."

"You still got your son," Cappy said.

"I guess you could say that."

"I lost my son."

"I know you did. I hate that, Cappy."

"So do I."

"You get out much, Cap?"

"Nope. No reason to."

"Maybe it'll get better."

"No, it won't get no better. You oughta know that."

"I keep wondering whether it's finished."

"It's finished."

"How do you know?"

"They ain't nothin' worth doin'."

"It seems like that, all right."

"You came back to North Albany."

"I did," said Edward.

"What for?"

"No place else to go."

"That's a good reason. So long, Eddie."

Cappy turned toward his house and Edward thought: Now Main Street has two hermits. He walked to Jack McCall's saloon for an ale. Respite. But maybe not. The night he moved back to Main Street he stopped at Jack's for an ale. Smiler McMahon and Petey Parker were at the bar when he came up beside them.

"Something stinks," Petey said.

"Yeah. We don't need that around here," Smiler said, and he and Petey crossed the room and sat at a table.

"I'll have an ale," Edward said to the bartender, a man he didn't know, but who obviously took his cue from Smiler.

"One's all you get," said the bartender.

Edward let him draw the ale. He picked it up and poured it onto the floor, then let the glass drop and shatter in the puddle.

Now, through the screen door, he saw Jimmy McGrath behind the bar. Four men looked at him when he entered, then went back to their beer. Had he ceased stinking after only a month?

"What'll it be, Eddie?" Jimmy asked.

"I'll try an ale. The last glass I had here I never got to drink."

"I heard about that," Jimmy said. "And so did Jack. He fired that stupid son of a bitch. 'Nobody tells Eddie Daugherty he can't drink in my saloon,' Jack said."

Jimmy set an ale in front of Edward, then sat on his stool behind the bar.

"Here's to Jack," Edward said, taking a mouthful. "I thought you retired, Jim."

"I did. Had two toes taken off from the sugar. But I come in nights when Jack needs help. Business is kinda quiet, and I'm next door. Long as I don't stand up too long."

"The whole neighborhood's quiet."

"Right. But the Tablet Company's comin' in up the road. They're hiring men, and women too, they say."

"That'll be good for business."

Edward took another mouthful of ale.

"Eddie," said Jimmy, "I'm sorry about the fire, and your wife. They hit you hard."

"That they did."

"I remember her coming in after some ale when Emmett was dying. I didn't serve her first, but she kept at me. She knew what she wanted, that one."

"You could say that," Edward said.

"The fire take everything, did it?"

"I saved some journals, inside a trunk in the cellar. They got wet but I can read them. A few books, some silver, odds and ends, a piece of marble. The rest is ashes."

"How you gonna live now?"

"That's a hell of a question, Jimmy."

"People know you're holed up down there in the house. They see the ice and the food going in. Freddy Doran, the mailman, says the letters he delivers are gone outa the box the next day."

"I don't read letters. They're all about yesterday."

"We got a letter here for you," Jimmy said.

He went to the back bar and opened a drawer, handed a letter to Edward.

"Came about a month ago. 'Hold for pickup,' it says."

When Jimmy drew beer for the men down the bar, Edward looked at the letter. Maginn's hand. He opened it.

Old Chum Edward,

Missed you at your opening night. If you're up for a bit of a chat, look me up at 65 Division Street, any time. Always a pleasure to see you.

M

Edward pocketed the letter, finished his ale.

"Another?" Jimmy asked.

"I'll move along," Edward said.

"Anything I can do, say the word," said Jimmy.

"If I ever figure out the word I'll let you know."

He walked back to Main Street and climbed the stairs to his workroom. He noted the time, nine-forty-five on the mantel clock, as he picked up the revolver from the desk. He put it in his back pocket and walked down the stairs, feeling the bulk of the pistol, opened the front door and stepped onto the porch. He stared at the long shadows the trees made on Main Street's bricks, at the sky incandescent with moonlight. The brilliant blackness was suffusing his being like an elixir of resolution. He took the pistol from his pocket and stared at it. He saw Emmett's finger on the trigger. There is a reason for everything.

He walked into the house and through the hallway to the kitchen, down the back steps and across the yard to Emmett's toolshed. He found matches and candle and lit them. He saw Emmett's vise covered with dust. He broke open the pistol and let the six bullets fall onto the workbench. He opened the vise jaws and put the pistol barrel between them, tightened the jaws. He took down a small sledgehammer from its hook and swung, then swung it again, and again, until the pistol broke in three pieces. He opened the vise jaws, tossed the pieces and the bullets into the trash bucket.

Giles, Felicity, and I bring you greetings even so, Maginn.

EDWARD GOES TO THE TENDERLOIN AT A LATE HOUR

DIVISION STREET, FIVE blocks long, ran west from Quay Street on the river, then crossed Broadway, Liberty, Dallius, and Green Streets, which at this hour formed a neighborhood grid thrumming with the revels and lusts of the night city. This was Albany's Tenderloin, and life was open, the streets full of motion, the Palace Lodging House catering to quick turnover, Scambelluri's and Marino's poolrooms, side by side, both busy, Dorgan's Good Life Saloon, which called itself a concert hall, thriving on music for illegal dancing, for thou shalt not dance in a saloon in Albany. And on the stoops of houses with telltale awnings on their windows (business was so good Jidgie Shea had opened an awning shop on the street), whores of the white race, and one *mulata* on the stoop of the Creole house, were taking the air this stifling night; and together they formed a tableau of discrete enticements. Youths too poor to buy any of their offerings walked Division Street, hoping for a charitable glimpse of raised thigh, unsequestered breast.

"Come and get it," one whore said to Edward. "Anything you want you can find right here. You don't find it, you ain't lookin' for it."

Sixty-five Division Street, a three-story brick dwelling, gave entrance off street level. It adjoined the Good Life, and Edward heard the saloon piano and banjo ringing out a ragtime melody he could put no name to as he rang the bell. A well-shaped woman in her forties, wearing high-necked blouse and long, black skirt, greeted him. Edward flashed that she should have one crossed eye, but she did not.

"You looking for company?" she asked.

"I'm looking for Maginn. Is he here?"

"He's here," she said, gesturing for Edward to enter.

"My name is Edward Daugherty."

"I know who you are."

"How is that possible?"

"He talks about you."

Maginn *talks* about you, of course. He plots to destroy you. Why didn't you know this the instant Giles blew Felicity into naked infinity? Who profited from that explosion? Yes, the cur Cully was a likely avenger. But when myopia wanes, Maginn, without doubt, emerges as the epiphanic presence at the slaughter. And you, Edward, the true target, you couldn't see that; you and Maginn such great friends, brothers of the ink stain, comrades of the imagination. Gainsaying fool is what you were. Now here you stand, believing you can goad evil into explaining itself, wondering what the whore of justice looks like, wallowing in your pathetic desire to mean.

"He's at the bar," the woman said, and led the way to a large parlor furnished with two sofas and three armchairs of dark red plush, a scatter of Oriental rugs, maroon drapes on the two windows, and lighted by four electrified gas lamps with pale-blue taffeta shades. Music and tobacco smoke came through a half-open door that led to the dance floor of the saloon (Edward could see two women and two men dancing), and at the small bar at the end of the parlor a very young, carrot-haired woman, wearing a blouse that covered little of her large, shapely breasts, was pouring liquor for a man in shirtsleeves who was smoking the butt of a thin cigar. Maginn.

"Ah, Daugherty, you worthless mutt," Maginn said, "you're here at last. You look well for a man whose life has been destroyed."

"You don't look well at all, Maginn. You look shriveled. You look like a chimney sweep's brush. Are you dying?"

"Aren't we all? But I'll live out the week."

Maginn had lost hair on his head and had blackened his mustache. His skin was sallow and he was thinner by fifteen pounds from Edward's last vision of him. A broomstraw of a man, probably venereally ravaged. His sickly look delighted Edward.

"Have you met Nell?" Maginn asked.

The woman who'd brought Edward in stood next to Maginn.

"Nell runs this emporium," Maginn said. "She's also my wife, my strong right arm, my favorite toss, and a font of money and strumpet wisdom. I love her like a sister. I'd be lost without her. Do you remember her?"

Edward looked at Nell and again recognized something but did not know what.

"You met in that tenebrous tent city we visited during the State Fair. You fancied her and she you, but you went forward to a more elderly crotch, while I regressed to the nubile Nell, a relationship that's endured for, what is it now, sweet suck of my life, twenty-seven years, on and off? Nell remembers *you*, Edward. I reminded her how she upped her skirt for you. Would you up it again, Nell? Give him a new look at the old puss?"

"He looks like a real gentleman, is what I say. Such fine duds he's got. The genuine article."

"A gentleman, oh yes." And Maginn, visibly perturbed by the remark, turned to the barmaid. "And this is Cherry. Say hello to Edward, Cherry."

"Howdja do, Edward," Cherry said.

Edward smiled at Cherry.

"And pour him a brandy, the best we have for this *gentleman*. Cherry, Edward, played the twelve-year-old virgin in the last house she worked. But she swiftly aged into this million-dollar set of tits, with only irony for a hymen. Does Cherry interest you, Edward?"

Edward said nothing.

"Let the gentleman sit down with his drink," Nell said. "Let him get a word in."

"Of course. Sit, Edward, sit. Get a word in, if you have any left after that theatrical debacle."

Edward and Maginn sat in the plush, facing each other.

"Gentleman. You called him a gentleman," Maginn said to Nell.

"This is Eddie, a mick to the heel of his boot, transformed by adroit social maneuvering into the elite, affluent Edward Daugherty, Esquire, famous playwright, a bit infamous lately, though. He recently had a major opening night with his new play, staged with considerable fanfare at the Hall. But, alas, it was only another facade, a mongoloid mishmash, an ambitious botch that closed with a wail and a snivel after one performance. My condolences, Edward. Did you like my critique of it?"

"At what point did you become an assassin, Maginn?"

"Uh-oh, he's getting personal, Nell. Time for the parade, get a bit of life in this party."

Nell left the room, and Maginn dropped his cigar into the spittoon by his chair, then coughed and spat into it, the spew of rotted lungs, Edward hoped.

"You haven't touched your drink, Edward, and you seem depressed. I can't blame you, given the burden you carry, some of it my doing, I fear. Truly sorry, old fellow. I berate myself constantly for what I did. You can see how I'm suffering here. But listen, when you see the parade you'll perk up, old Edward Edward Edward. But tell the truth, now. Isn't that name a sham all by itself? Why not call yourself Eduardo, or Edmundo, or Oedipus, for chrissake? You always went for older women, didn't you? Why not just be Eddie, like other micks? Edward exudes pretense. But I'll wager it wears well in your social set."

"You invented a brilliant scheme, Maginn—bravura insight into the very worst human impulses. And I actually might've died, except for Giles's faulty aim."

"I appreciate the compliment," Maginn said, "but you overestimate my intention. It *was* a clever scheme, and I revel at the genius in it. But I was only answering Giles's little joke—at least you got *that* right in your wretched melodrama. Who knew Giles harbored such violence? I saw him as one of the more gentle bigots of his tribe. Remember his joke about the Irishman whose cousin suffered two heart attacks and died, and the mick asked, 'Did he die of the first attack or the second?' Giles enjoyed jokes at the expense of others. A pity he didn't live to enjoy mine.

"My plan was to repay your joke with my own, but then Giles decides to atomize the useless Felicity bitch, and his own vapid self.

What an oblique bonanza! Sorry he got a bit of you in the doing, but look at you! You've recovered splendidly. And I knew our lovely Melissa would survive, of course. The world loves soiled innocents, when they're beautiful and repentant of their sin. Melissa, it must be said, repents well, but doesn't know what sin is, wouldn't you agree?"

"I'm surprised she's not here working for you."

"She's beyond my means and always was," said Maginn. "But not beyond yours. Did you know she put Cully up to that rape of Felicity? Perverse little twat. She told Cully she'd be his if he'd rape Felicity with her looking on. She wanted to watch, and then comfort the poor, ravaged victim."

"More lies, Maginn."

"Cully told me this himself the day he left New York. I was with him before and after his little orgy. I even put him on the road with that story about the Albany police being after him. It was time to be rid of the lowlife pest. Didn't Melissa tell you any of this? I was with her too, earlier that day. In your room."

"If your fiction was half as imaginative as your lies, Maginn, you'd have been famous years ago."

"You don't know the truth when you hear it, Edward. You never did. But forget that and cop a sneak at these wenches."

Nell entered ahead of three women, drew Cherry into the head of the line, then stood aside and let the four whores parade for Edward. Cherry opened her blouse, raised her offerings with her hands.

"We have two more in the stable," Maginn said, "but they're busy at the moment," and he walked to the second whore and caressed her belly. "This one carries her snake-head dildo at the ready and wears an Egyptian headdress, suitable for the moving pictures. I call her Putonalissa. A French artist I met in New Orleans sketched her costume for me on a bar towel."

"New Orleans," Edward said. "When you went down to settle up with Cully?"

The remark stopped Maginn's spiel, and he gave Edward a twisted look; then continued.

"This young lady with the mask and open robe we call Complicity," he said, parting the whore's robe with both hands. "Sweet young thing, but she carries a whip. You don't know what to expect from Complicity."

The third whore, a blonde, wore only a gown of transparent white chiffon, and Maginn lifted the chiffon to pat her bush. "You probably guessed the name of this fair-haired beauty already," he said. "The lovely Beatrina, our *pièce de résistance,* by far our prettiest, and most angelic. I'd say her dress was suitable for a trip to Paradise, or even a walk down the old church aisle."

Edward drank his brandy in two gulps to be rid of it. Maginn, seething with archaic rage against the divine arbiter of talent, trying to commit murder-by-whores to avenge his meager inheritance of the myth, droned on, urging the women to display themselves, even Nell, who did up her skirt, and whose freckled thighs, Edward thought with faded memory, had widened since the State Fair.

"So there you have it, Edward. Which one would cheer you most? Or would you like two? Or all five? It's on the house, you know."

The whores seated themselves on the sofa to await Edward's decision and Cherry went back to the bar, her blouse askew. Nell poured Edward a new brandy and brought it to him. He sipped it, smiled at Maginn.

"I can't tell you how much it's meant, Maginn, seeing all this," he said. "Ever since I met you I've overpraised you, especially that beastly fiction no one ever published. I got you a job you weren't equal to, and even abided your envious tirades. I concluded you were the eternally inadequate man, *Homo invidiosus,* but all things keep striving for that higher form that nature designs for them, and I see tonight that you've climbed up from pigsty to pimpdom, up from creative myth to a career in vice, up from skulking whorehound to grand cuntmaster with a troop of trollops. Do you like that phrase? It's very Maginnish. Vaudeville tonight! The Grand Cuntmaster Maginn and His Troop of Twisted Trollops. One night only! When the matter is ready the form will come, as I've been saying for years, Maginn, and you've evolved into absolute parity with nullity. In any world worth inhabiting, you now mean nothing at all."

"Very good, Edward, very droll. Are you finished?"

"Not quite. There's Cully's confession that you incited Giles to murder. Poor Cully. He asked you for bail money and you failed him."

"I didn't have it. And there is no confession."

"True, his confession disappeared from the New Orleans police files, in the same way you disappeared when police came to *The Argus* to ask you about Cully. But my investigator turned up the detective who took Cully's confession, and he's got his notes and he'll testify. So will Clubber. So will I. And I wouldn't put it past Melissa to put in a good word for you. My man also found a fellow who says Cully's killers were paid to hang him, paid by somebody who looked like you."

"You're pathetic, Daugherty."

"I often tell myself that. Even so, I've documented this, and when I got your letter I gave my report to *The Argus*. They'll print it this week, with an editorial urging the case be reopened."

Maginn picked up the spittoon beside his chair and heaved its cigar butts, slops, and globs of phlegm in Edward's face. Edward snatched the spittoon from Maginn's hand and swung it in a back-handed smash against his head. As Maginn staggered, Edward swung forward and smashed him full in the face, and Maginn's face exploded with blood.

"Nell!" Maginn called up out of his weakness, collapsed sideways over his armchair, spitting out pieces of broken teeth, "Nell, do him! Do him!"

Edward turned to look for Nell and saw her right arm swinging a piece of lead pipe. It hit high on the left side of his head, and as he went down he saw Cherry moving toward him with a rag and a bottle of what he already knew was their chloroform.

EDWARD WAKES IN THE MOONLIGHT AT THREE O'CLOCK IN THE MORNING

HE FELT THE tongue on his face and thought of a deer at the salt lick. He'd been walking down the sloping corridor after Katrina and saw steam shovels moving great slabs of broken marble to block the exit. The way out now was down, down the high, grassy slope past the broken statuary. It led him to the edge of a high precipice over an abyss, and he felt the onset of his vertigo. A finger touched his outer thigh and he turned to see the beautiful young whore. "Pressure makes it pop out," she said. "You're less of a sybarite these days, but nobody cares. The sinners are too chaotic." He realized the paper he'd had in his hand was missing. He looked where it might have fallen, then saw it in his other hand. He touched his hip. His wallet was gone, as was the whore, and he knew that from here forward, something would vanish with every breath he took.

He opened his eye into pain and moonlight and the breath of the animal licking his hair. Will it bite my face? He closed his eye, felt in the dirt and found a small glass bottle at his fingertips. He dug it out and knew from its shape it once held paregoric. The planet Neptune was discovered by mathematical analysis of the movement of another planet. Such has happened. The tongue is a dog, not a deer, licking my pain. He licked his own lips and realized the dog was licking his blood. He tasted a sweetness that was not blood. The chloroform. He raised his hand and swiped the dog's jaw with the bottle. The animal yelped and Edward opened an eye to see it standing off, waiting. It barked once. Edward growled and the dog ran, a whelp.

He could see tall weeds, but the earth was bare and moist beneath his face, and smelled of ashes. The pain was an ax blade. He did not recognize the weeds or the buildings beyond them. He knew only the moon, and the heat of the dark, early morning, and the burned earth where his cheek touched it. He raised his head into new pain that might kill him. If it did not, he would raise himself. Do not go too fast. Up, and roll. Now sit. He saw light in an upper room of a house, another light at street level. By the light of the moon he saw that the weeds around him had grown over, and through, charred remnants of trash. He closed his eyes to see how to get down the precipice to where Katrina was.

The light at street level came from a window whose painted lettering announced "Saloon." Edward saw two men talking with the barkeep. He pushed open the half door, went to the bar.

"A double whiskey."

"Christ, what happened to you?"

"Somebody hit me with a pipe."

"You know who did it?"

"A woman I knew a long time ago."

"They don't forget, do they?" the barman said.

He wet a towel and handed it to Edward.

"Wipe your face, pal."

Edward took the towel while the barman poured whiskey. The blood on the towel was abundant, streaked white with ashes. He wiped his eyes, his mouth. He drank the whiskey, returned the glass for a refill.

"What street is this?" he asked.

"Dallius."

"How far are we from Division?"

"Three blocks."

"They didn't carry me far."

"Who didn't?"

"You know a place called the Good Life?"

"Dorgan's. They closed early tonight."

"How do you know?"

"I'm gettin' their regulars."

Edward drank the second whiskey. The barman gave him another wet towel. He wiped his ear, blotted his head, blood still oozing. How much had he lost?

"You wanna go the hospital? I'll get a cop'll take ya," the barman said.

"I'll go later. What do I owe you?" He reached into his pocket, wallet gone. "I can't pay you. They robbed me."

"You had a big night."

"I'll come back and pay."

"If you ever get home. You want another shot?"

"The pain is terrific."

"Have another."

Edward drank his third double.

"What's your name?" he asked.

"Grady."

"You're a man worth knowing, Grady. If I don't die I'll be back. Can I keep this towel?"

"Take a new one."

He wet a third towel for Edward.

"I'll pay your laundry bill, too," Edward said.

He walked up Dallius toward where Division crossed. The pain was awful but easing. Why did he want to go back to the whorehouse? Explain the riddle of the goat. He turned on Division and walked until he came to Dorgan's. It was dark. He broke a panel of the glass door with a high kick and entered. By the light of the streetlamp he saw the back bar empty of bottles. He walked across the dance floor toward Maginn's, opened the whorehouse door, and stepped into darkness. He found a window and raised a shade, letting in light from the street. The rugs, lamps, chairs, and drapes were all gone. One sofa and small bar, without bottles, remained. He moved the bar and found nothing on its one shelf. They took the lead pipe and the chloroform. On the floor he found a large envelope.

He went outside and left the front door wide open. Let the rats out. On the street he lightly touched his wound. The blood seemed to be coagulating. He stood under the streetlight and opened the envelope, to find two dozen identical postcard photos of a woman in a flat, flowered hat, black stockings, shoes, and a white blouse she was holding partly open. She wore no skirt and was facing front, taking the viewer's picture with her fluffy black camera. Nellie. He would recognize those thighs anywhere. He pocketed one postcard, tossed the rest.

He walked toward the all-night cabstand on State Street, evaluating his latest creation: Cully's lost confession. Not until he'd finished his monologue to Maginn had he thought of resurrecting it. He'd often imagined an investigator would discover it just that way; and it also made perfect sense for Maginn to hire Cully's hangman.

His mood improved as he thought of Maginn, with fewer teeth, and fettered with whores, forced into midnight exile by the power of fiction.

EDWARD CONCLUDES A DIALOGUE WITH KATRINA ON HIS FRONT PORCH

EDWARD REACHED FOR his watch when the intern at St. Peter's Hospital finished with his bandage. The watch was gone. What else could he lose tonight? The pain in his head was horrible, the whiskey wearing off, the powders they gave him not yet working. They wanted him to stay overnight in the hospital but he would not. He wanted to walk to Main Street but he lacked the stamina. They rang for a cab and the intern gave him a chair. He sat by the door and waited for the cab.

He looked for Giles in the hospital hallway but did not find him. He's here someplace. He saw a wall clock that said four-twenty. It's early. Late. It was not likely that his play would be resurrected. His playwriting days were over. Everything was over. It won't get no better, Cappy said. Nothin' worth doin', it's finished. The only thing that isn't over is the pain. He regretted not having time enough to do the play properly, and to use the real names. Who would care? The play would never be done again. But if it was done, some scenes would be different.

(KATRINA *is seated on sofa in the Daugherty drawing room, looking at photo album.* EDWARD *stands with his arms folded, watching her. They are dressed for the evening. She wears a corsage of violets.)*

EDWARD: You could never admit your behavior was unacceptable.

KATRINA: Of course I could. I just said you had to accept it. I understood *your* behavior perfectly. You were correct in moving to New York. I was impossible.

EDWARD: You're very understanding of your own contradictions.

KATRINA: I would've gone mad otherwise.

EDWARD: You can seem as mad as the Queen of Bedlam. The soul obsessed by primal passions, trying to carry out the divine will. That's *Peer Gynt* but it's you.

(KATRINA *picks up photo album, raises it for* EDWARD *to see.)*

KATRINA: Yes, *Peer Gynt.* Look at this wonderful picture of Adelaide and me up at Schroon Lake. What a wonderful summer that was. It was my fault she died.

EDWARD: More madness. You stay alive through the death of others. Pain and guilt, romantic despair, the tragic dimension. If you'd abandon this melodrama and let the dead stay dead, we'd be happier.

KATRINA: I should have died in the Delavan.

EDWARD: I should have died when Giles shot me.

KATRINA: Giles wasn't your fault. You behaved admirably during that terrible episode. Admirably.

EDWARD: I behaved like a fool, the only way I knew how. Look at me, Katrina. Leave the dead. Let's salvage the time left to us.

(KATRINA *walks to the drawing room mirror, looks at her reflection.)*

KATRINA: How much time do we have, Edward?

(EDWARD *comes up behind her, looks into the mirror over her shoulder.*)

EDWARD: You know more than I about such things.

(KATRINA *turns and faces* EDWARD, *their faces very close.*)

KATRINA: If I fainted now, would you unpin my corsage? Would you undo the buttons of my bodice to help me breathe?

When the cab was halfway down Main Street, Edward saw he had left a light on in the parlor. His pain was leveling, but would not go away. He went to the bedroom for money he kept in a jar, paid the driver, then went to the icebox. The ice was almost gone. With the pick he chipped some ice into a glass, then half-filled the glass with whiskey. Quarter to five. The whiskey and powders would take away the pain. He stared out the kitchen window at the canal and remembered Emmett in his days as the lock tender, standing here watching the boat traffic, waiting for trouble and grievance from the canalers, his problem as well as theirs to solve. It may be that the existence of the planet Neptune does not contradict the design of the solar system. How can it if it is really there?

Edward walked out the back door to Emmett's toolshed and found the bullets and broken pieces of the pistol in the waste bucket. He picked them out and carried them to the kitchen.

"Did you ever consider," he said to Emmett, "that I never was the Irishman on horseback? It may be I was free of racial and social destinies, and that what I wanted was altogether different from what had gone before."

He put the bullets and pistol on the kitchen table, where Hughie Gahagan would have been sitting. The dead pistol meant something simple: sycophancy, scorn, false praise, cruelty, rage, narcissism, pain, prayer. Maginn was innocent of everything relating to success. He contrived complexity as a substitute for disuse. "If you don't find her in one room, try the other," he wrote on his note with the passkey.

It may be that after the worst has happened, you see that Neptune was there from the beginning, problematically, and the old orbit of death is superseded. Then you see that faith, or its mathematical equivalent, has to do with your discovery.

When Emmett wanted anything he invoked Connacht.

Booming voice.

Shorn of sustenance, shorn of the past, of love, of the theater of action, what's left to a man? The answer, son, is the necessary sin. You won't name it. It's written in a forgotten code. The light's still on in the parlor.

(The FIREMAN, *a handkerchief over his mouth and nose, carries* KATRINA *out of the burning house in his arms and crosses the street to where* EDWARD *is standing. The* FIREMAN *lays her down on the street, unbuttons her bodice, puts smelling salts under her nose. She does not move. The* FIREMAN *puts his mouth on hers, breathes into her. She opens her eyes, looks at the* FIREMAN, *then looks past him at* EDWARD, *who moves closer to her.)*

KATRINA: I can see you.

EDWARD: I thought you were lost.

(The FIREMAN *lifts himself away from* KATRINA *and exits. He waves at her as he goes.* EDWARD *kneels beside* KATRINA, *raises her head and kisses her.)*

KATRINA: I remember a poem, a woman dying in her lover's arms. She has come down from the mountain of gold and as he holds her she turns to ashes.

EDWARD: You won't die, Katrina. It's wrong to die now. You won't die, Katrina. You won't die.

KATRINA: Life is something that should not have been.

EDWARD: I loved life when you loved me.

KATRINA: I loved you?

(Pause.)

Quite likely. I forget.

*(*KATRINA *dies in his arms.)*

Edward picked up his whiskey and walked to the front porch. He sat in the chair beside Emmett and decided mockery was a more exalted mode of behavior than was generally assumed. He sat on the porch drinking whiskey with Emmett until he grew ravenous. He thought of what he would cook.

He would fry bacon.

He would stay up and outlast Emmett. He had outlasted Martin, and the boy went back to New York. That was part of their problem. The father's energy acknowledged the irrelevance of the future, the worship of the present tense.

He could almost smell the bacon. A pig is turned into bacon, bacon becomes food that gives unity and purpose to the imagination. Brother William died in the fire, kneeling, turned into a bent cinder. Katrina, heroine of neighborhood children, had walked into the classroom and whipped William with the same stick he'd been using to whip a boy. Katrina understood the nature of fire.

Edward, seeing the earliest blue line of things to come, finished his whiskey. Then he went to the icebox for the bacon, which will always be with us.